Little Pieces: This Side of Japan

Stories by Michael Hoffman

This book is a work of fiction. Any resemblance to actual events or persons, living or dead, is entirely coincidental.

"Little Pieces: This Side of Japan," by Michael Hoffman. ISBN 978-1-60264-605-6 (softcover); 978-1-60264-606-3 (ebook).

Published 2010 by Virtualbookworm.com Publishing Inc., P.O. Box 9949, College Station, TX 77842, US. ©2010, Michael Hoffman. All rights reserved. No part of this publication may be reproduced, stored in a retrieval system, or transmitted in any form or by any means, electronic, mechanical, recording or otherwise, without the prior written permission of Michael Hoffman.

Manufactured in the United States of America.

Contents

Author's Note i

First Snow 1

Dragonflies 17

The Miracle 77

Sonoko 111

The Concussion 125

Little Pieces 157

Author's Note

Fate, I guess you'd call it, placed me in Japan at a certain impressionable stage of my life, and I've been here ever since. That's why my stories are set in Japan – not the Japan of the Japanese, not quite the Japan of the non-Japanese, maybe nobody's Japan but mine.

"First Snow" and "Sonoko" first appeared in The Japan Times.

Michael Hoffman,
Hokkaido 2010

First Snow

"Tamaki-kun! It's you, isn't it?"

Startled, the man looked up from the book he'd been perusing. He stared at the woman in bewilderment. "Yes, my name is Tamaki..."

"And you don't recognize me!"

"I...no... I'm sorry..."

The woman seemed amused rather than offended, as though the man's failure to recognize her was even more delightful than their unexpected meeting. She smiled; her eyes twinkled mischievously. "Will you take a chance and come with me anyway?"

"Go with you! Where?"

"For a cup of coffee. My treat. There's a coffee shop one floor down. We won't even have to go out. Is it still snowing, I wonder? Imagine snow this early in the season! What's this?" She took the book from his hands. "A history of India! Are you interested in India?"

"I'm thinking of going there."

"Business or pleasure?"

He shrugged vaguely. Opening the book at random, she read, "'India's largest concentration of temples, in Bhu...' something-or-other... 'was constructed over many centuries by a succession of...' Oh, look!" She showed him a color photograph that suddenly struck her: a gleaming golden temple, its reflection shimmering in water.

"That's the Golden Temple at Amritsar."

"Quite the connoisseur, I see. Are you going to buy the book?"

"I don't know, I…"

"Oh, buy it, it looks so interesting!" She made a movement as though to take it to the cash herself, but Tamaki in confusion cried out, "Wait!"

"Well, put it back then, and let's go for coffee. You can come back for it later."

———

They seated themselves at a table by the window. Outside, the snow fell in fat, lazy flakes. To the waitress, who appeared almost immediately, the woman said, "Cappuccino, please," and then looked questioningly at her companion, who nodded as though affirming some inner thought and mumbled, "Mm."

"Tamaki-kun! Really, I'm so happy… but you still don't know who I am! Oh, but this is… Wouldn't it be nice to just spend an hour together like this, me knowing you but you not knowing me? But I'm sure you'd recognize me long before the hour was up. No? Nothing? You look at me and see a perfect stranger, nothing more? Can I have changed so much in thirty years?"

"Thirty years! Thirty years ago I was six years old!"

"And I was seventeen. There, I've confessed my age. If you care to flatter me and tell me you'd never have guessed, I won't mind. Think,

Tamaki-kun, think! Who babysat for you that time your father had a gall bladder operation and your mother – "

"Sayoko-chan!"

"Ah, thank you." The waitress had returned with their coffee. There was a moment's silence while she laid down their cups, and then:

"Sayoko-chan! But... how can you possibly have recognized me? I'm bald..."

"Oh, baldness changes a man much less than men seem to think. Besides, I saw you at your father's funeral."

"You were at my father's funeral?"

"Yes."

"Well then, why didn't you come over and speak to us? Mother would have been so pleased."

"I'm not so sure of that." She smiled faintly. "But tell me about yourself! What have you been up to all these years? What have you made of yourself? I'm dying to know."

"What have I made of myself? Nothing." He shrugged and gave a somewhat forced laugh. "Whatever potential I may have shown at six, I failed to live up to."

"Oh, come! You're still young! Your life has barely begun!"

"No doubt. What about you? You're married, of course?"

"Why 'of course'?"

"Single, then."

"It would seem to follow, but no, not that either. I was married twice. Once divorced and

3

now… I don't know what I am! My husband and I live in the same house, we exchange greetings every now and then… Is that marriage? Well, maybe it is. And you?"

"I'm single."

"More and more people are nowadays."

"Actually" – Tamaki's face brightened at the memory – "it was you I wanted to marry."

"When you were six. I remember."

"You said, 'If you want to marry me you'd better get a sword.' I said, 'Why?' And you said, 'Because my boyfriend will challenge you to a duel, and you'll have to fight him for me.' Remember?"

"I do!"

They were silent for a time, looking into each other's faces and smiling.

"Would I ever have guessed who you were?" he mused dreamily. "It seems so obvious now. Why, you've hardly changed at all!"

"Tamaki-kun, listen. I can't stay, I'm meeting someone for lunch in an hour. Why don't you come to my place for dinner tonight? We can get a little drunk, talk over old times… Or are you already spoken for, this last Sunday of the year?"

"No, but… what about your husband?"

"My husband is in Manila. He travels all over the world. For business and pleasure. Don't worry about him. We'll be quite alone."

"No children?"

"A daughter, married and living in New Zealand."

"Well…"

"Say yes, Tamaki-kun. It's so dreary all alone in that big house."

"Well... yes then. With pleasure. Shall I bring white wine or red?"

"Surprise me."

———

They sat side by side on a long white couch, nursing their drinks – he scotch on the rocks, she vodka and tonic. By now whatever reserve there had been between them had melted away. They were simply old friends, lifelong friends, who had known each other since childhood. The fact that they had not seen each other in thirty years was forgotten. Tamaki marveled at the magnificence of the room he found himself in. It was like a drawing room in an old romance, with lighted candles, a small fire crackling on the hearth, and in the background, as though provided by an invisible private orchestra, soft, feathery chamber music. The savory odor of roasting meat wafted in from the kitchen.

"It's funny," she was saying. "You can always tell when it's snowing outside, even when the curtains are drawn and everything else about the outside world, including the damp and cold, has altogether vanished from your mind. Do you see what I mean?"

"Yes," he said, smiling blissfully, though in fact he had scarcely taken in her words. It all seemed so unreal. Sayoko-chan! He sipped his scotch. How many glasses had he drunk? He must be careful. When he drank too much he was not immune to being sick to his stomach – and what an awful end that would be to such a beautiful, beautiful evening!

They brought each other up to date on their life histories. She was, she said, "a second-rate jazz singer," performing at "second-rate clubs" in Tokyo and occasionally elsewhere in the country. She laughed now at her childhood pretensions of having serious talent. Her disillusion had been traumatic but not crushing. Did it matter, after all, if she wasn't a star? Her singing might not please the most discriminating ears, but it was good enough for the easygoing audiences who came to see her. If she failed to shake people to the core of their being, she at least made them happy, "after a fashion, for a passing moment… It's funny," she said again. "More than once over the years I imagined I'd look out into the audience and see you sitting there."

"I'll come. You sang to me when I was little. I remember."

He told her in turn of his attempt, and failure, to follow in his father's footsteps. His father had been a distinguished journalist – an investigative reporter in his early years, and later on managing editor of the notoriously hard-hitting Maiasa Shimbun. His father's position assured him a place at the newspaper, and at first he showed no small degree of promise. Writing under a pen name in order to come out from under his father's shadow, he established himself as a respected commentator on global politics. But then, he said, suddenly it all fell apart.

"What happened?"

"I suddenly realized... I didn't know what I was talking about. I was merely *pretending* to know, using highly sophisticated language (I was good at that) to hide my ignorance. My opinions, my world view, were built on sand."

"I suppose we all – "

"One day I wrote a column of sheer nonsense, learned-sounding gibberish. I did it on purpose. I'm not sure what possessed me, but... well, I did it. And do you know what? Nobody noticed! It got past the page editor, past the proofreader... and later that week there were three letters to the editor from readers who thought it brilliant, provocative, 'intellectually daring' – yes, one reader actually used those very words. 'Intellectually daring'!"

"Well?"

"I gave myself the weekend to think it over, and on Monday... I submitted my resignation."

"Your resignation! For that?"

"Yes! For that!"

"When? How long ago?"

"In October."

"You've been out of work since October?"

"Yes, Sayoko-chan. I've been out of work since October."

"But what will you do? You can't simply..."

"I don't know. One thing I thought of was to go to India and... just see what happens..."

After dinner she accepted his offer to help clean up, and when the dishes had been washed, dried and put away she said, "You don't have to leave yet, do you?"

"No, I'm in no hurry."

"Shall we have another glass of wine?"

"By all means."

"I can't tell you how much pleasure this evening has given me, Tamaki-kun."

"Me too. It's wonderful seeing you again, Sayoko-chan."

"And this won't be the last time, will it? I mean... now that we've found each other, we can be friends – can't we?"

"Of course. We *are* friends."

"Let's go into the living room."

He followed her to the window, where she drew back the curtain slightly and exclaimed, "Oh, look!" The snow was falling thick and fast, though gently. "Look how white everything is! Do you like snow, Tamaki-kun?"

"I hate to disappoint you and say no, but... well, no." He laughed. It was such a ringing, childlike laugh that he himself was startled by it.

"Come, let's sit down. A glass of white wine, in honor of the snow. Tamaki-kun... I want to tell you something. May I?"

He laughed again. "Do you need my permission? Granted!"

"Yes, I do need your permission."

He noticed with surprise her strange gravity. "What is it?"

"I'm... I don't... I..."

"What is it, Sayoko-chan? Tell me."

"I don't *have* to tell you this, nothing *compels* me... if I keep it to myself there is no way in the world you would ever find out, or even suspect... it would never cross your mind..."

He was all concern now. "Sayoko, what's upsetting you? Was it something I said? Sometimes when I've had a bit to drink I..."

"No! No, nothing like that. As I said, I don't *have* to tell you this, and I'm not altogether sure myself why... suddenly... But suddenly, you see, it somehow feels *right* to tell you, and... and wrong not to. May I proceed?"

"Please do, if it'll ease your mind."

She sipped her wine. "Your father... when I was seventeen..."

He thought he saw her lower lip quiver, but a moment later he wasn't sure; if it did, she immediately recovered her self-possession.

"Your father seduced me. Or I seduced him. Or we seduced each other. Who knows how these things happen? I know only one thing: I loved him. Loved him madly, passionately. I've never loved anyone since. Maybe a girl has to be seventeen to really love a man. After that, the mist falls away, she sees life too clearly, she is no longer swept away by fantasy ... and fantasy... love is unthinkable without fantasy. Unthinkable. I was married twice, both times to good men, and yet... I was no longer seventeen. Have you

9

understood me, Tamaki-kun? From the expression on your face I'm not sure you have."

"I'm not sure I have either..." He was afraid he might be sick. Should he make a beeline for the toilet? He didn't know where it was, he would have to ask. It would be embarrassing, but the alternative was to stain this white couch, stain it grotesquely, irreparably; it wouldn't wash out, it would remain as a reminder, an eternal reminder... He rose unsteadily to his feet, took a deep breath, then another. "Let's go outside for a bit."

"Yes, let's!"

She seized his hand, in her enthusiasm pulling him forward with such force he almost stumbled, and the next thing he knew he was outside, filling his lungs with fresh, cold air, breathing it in in huge gulps. "Ah! Ah!" He turned and saw her behind him, her arms stretched out full length to the heavens and her mouth open, trying to catch the falling snow on her tongue.

"Isn't this beautiful, Tamaki-kun! Isn't it beautiful?" She laughed and laughed. "Oh, Tamaki-kun, it's so beautiful!"

The fresh air had steadied and sobered him. "We'll catch cold, it's freezing."

"Let's make a snowman!"

"No, Sayoko, we'd better go inside. We don't even have coats on."

The last train would already have left, and Sayoko pressed him to stay the night. When he demurred she said, "Do you have any idea how big this house is? To this day I sometimes get lost in it. There are twenty rooms you can choose from! Come into the kitchen, I'll make some coffee."

It was wonderful coffee, fresh, strong and hot. Closing his eyes, Tamaki sipped in silent appreciation.

She said, "You're not angry at me?"

"Angry? You know, I'll tell you something odd: I've never been angry in my life."

"Is that true? If so it's most unusual."

"It is true. My mother tells me that even as a baby I was never angry."

"How is your mother?"

"She's well."

"Still teaching tea ceremony?"

"Yes. Declining enrollment only fires her sense of mission. The more the times threaten to pass her by, the more..." He broke off suddenly, and looked hard at her. His silent, searching scrutiny seemed to go on a long time, until at last, lowering her eyes, she asked, "What is it?"

"When you said I should get a sword because your boyfriend would challenge me to a duel... did you... did you mean... my *father*?"

"No, Tamaki-kun!"

"No? But..."

"There was no *meaning* in that! It was just something funny to say to a six-year-old. Tamaki-kun! Listen to me, now. If you're going to get

11

angry for the first time in your life… don't let it be over that!"

"No, you're right, it would be silly, wouldn't it?" The silence thickened and seemed to envelop them. Closing his eyes, Tamaki could almost fancy he heard the snow falling outside.

"Sayoko-chan, did you tell me… what you told me… for a reason?"

She nodded.

"What is it?"

"I want us to be friends. Between friends there cannot be such a secret."

He awoke in a room flooded with sunlight and thought for an instant he was in India. No, not there – but where? Surveying his surroundings, he saw nothing familiar, nothing to help him get his bearings. Even filtered through a shoji paper screen, the sunshine seemed almost unnaturally bright. His head ached dully; there was something almost pleasant in the slight throbbing.

He lay back on the pillow and pulled the futon up to his chin; in spite of the sun it was quite cold. He closed his eyes and smiled to himself as he thought, "Does it matter where I am?"

He slept again, and dreamed of his father. He often did, and would awake with a distinct sense, so vivid were the dreams, of having paid his father a visit in the afterworld. Dead, it seemed,

his father was very much as he had been in life –
serenely strong, quietly wise. "You have to ignore
a great deal to feel that life is good," he liked to
say. "The miracle is that sometimes we can."

He awoke to find the sunlight fading. It was
evening already; he had slept all day! Surprise
cleared his head. He flung off the quilt, meaning
to dash downstairs and make his apologies, but
saw he was naked except for his drawers. Where
were his clothes? How odd – he had no memory
of undressing. On the other hand, what was odd
about it? "Drunk as I was, it's lucky I can
remember my own name!"

His clothes lay in a crumpled heap next to the
futon. In his haste he stumbled and almost
upended himself as he struggled to get into his
trousers. Managing at last, he rushed downstairs.
The kitchen and living room were deserted and
darkening in the gathering dusk. There were no
lights on, and no heat either; it was
uncomfortably chilly. Was Sayoko elsewhere in
the house, asleep perhaps? Had she gone out,
intending to be back soon? Or had she forgotten
him and left for the evening?

The telephone rang. He gasped as though at a
door being flung open by menacing strangers.
The sound, echoing through the silent empty
house, seemed unnaturally loud, but it gave no
clue as to where it was coming from. Where was
the phone? It rang and rang. Finally he found it,
on a little table in the hall – but should he answer
it? Maybe it was Sayoko calling to let him know
where she was and when she would be back; on

the other hand, supposing it was Sayoko's husband – what would he say? Or her daughter. No, impossible, he must not answer, it was out of the question. But the caller was evidently determined to get through. The ringing went on and on, growing more insistent, it seemed, with each ring, while Tamaki stood gaping at the phone in a kind of blank, numb astonishment.

He shook himself at last. "I'd better get out of here; where's my coat? Where did she put my coat?" He didn't know, having either forgotten or, more likely, not noticed. "Will that damn ringing ever stop? No one's home, no one's home!"

His shoes at best half on, he flung himself out of the house, pursued by the ringing telephone. Not even distance, it seemed, could muffle the sound. When finally he paused for breath he found himself at a swirling river, gleaming silver in the moonlight. He shivered. How strange. There were houses all around, many of them lighted up as though for an uncommonly jolly evening, but not a soul in the street of whom he could ask directions to the station. There was nothing to worry about, of course; a cruising taxi would come by eventually, or failing that, if he just kept walking he'd get his bearings sooner or later. Well, he'd better get started. It was too cold to simply stand there, coatless as he was.

And yet he lingered, as though hesitating over something. Closing his eyes, he seemed to feel a radiant warmth envelop him. He recognized it immediately for what it was – fever; but did it matter? It was such a delightful warmth; he needn't concern himself with the source of it. He felt something tickle his cheek. He opened his eyes and shivered. Snow. It was snowing again. The climate was changing; there was no accounting for the weather these days!

Was it true, what Sayoko had told him? Suppose it was. Did it change anything? Nothing. Everything was the same, exactly the same; he was now precisely what he had been before, a middle-aged man at loose ends – at hopelessly loose ends, indeed – and next week or the week after he'd be in India, a place as foreign to his experience and imagination as another planet. Yes, next week he'd be on another planet, another world, a world of golden temples gleaming under a searing sun. He closed his eyes and seemed to see them. And Sayoko... would Sayoko even exist, in that other world?

"What strange things are going through my mind! Strange thoughts, crazy almost..." Strangest of all was that he felt happy. There was no accounting for happiness at such a moment. He was feverish and lost, with no coat on, the snow falling more thickly every second. If he didn't start walking he would make himself seriously ill, perhaps even freeze to death, but though he saw this quite clearly he felt no inclination to move; everything seemed so perfect just as it was. "It's only when I open my eyes that I feel cold..."

Dragonflies

I

Hiranuma took off his glasses and lay his head down on his desk. He felt unaccountably sleepy. Should he yield to temptation and have a nap? Why not? He was alone in his own office, in his own house, where downstairs Shizuko, his wife, was dreamily playing a waltz or something on the piano. Maybe it was the music that was making him drowsy.

He was fifty-four years old. Of his youthful dreams of being a great writer, little had materialized. Still, all things considered, he had not done badly. He published this and that here and there, was respected if not lionized, and if his name failed to live on after his death, as almost surely it would – so what?

Akutagawa, now. There was a name to reckon with. Dead at thirty-five, a suicide, and yet eighty years later, who did not know him? Even those who had never read an Akutagawa story knew the name. He, Hiranuma, was at that moment engaged in writing an essay on him, an appreciation to mark the eightieth anniversary of his death. It was a problem, this essay he'd been commissioned to write. Rereading the master's stories, he was forced to ask himself: were they really so marvelous? Was there really so much more to them than jejune cleverness? When you waved away the smoke of verbal agility, was there any fire at the core?

What was that – the telephone? He shook off his torpor and listened. Yes, unmistakably, the phone was ringing downstairs. Shizuko, deep in her music, would not hear it. He would have to dash downstairs if he was not to miss the call; not that there was anyone he especially wanted to speak to. Still...

He fairly threw himself on the phone. "Hello!"

"Hiranuma? Is that you?"

Sawamoto, sounding just the faintest bit tipsy. "You working?"

"Not really."

"Come join me for a drink. I'm at the Cinnamon and Clover."

Why not? He was getting nowhere with the essay. "All right, give me an hour."

He hung up, went back upstairs and switched off the computer. What was the weather like? Summer was over but autumn had not yet begun. He gazed out the window at gray skies threatening rain. If only it *would* rain! It hadn't in weeks. Though there was no shortage of drinking water, Hiranuma felt the drought acutely; he felt parched, like the brownish grass and the withering flowers one saw in the neighborhood. He gazed beyond a line of ragged trees at the sea, gray as the sky and placid as a sheet of glass. It seemed to be waiting for something, expecting something... or was that just a literary figure of speech? "Time I gave up writing altogether," he murmured to himself. "Give up reading too. All I ever do is read and write, write and read. Hell with all that. Go out there and *live*, while there's still time. Do some *real* work for a change, physical work, handling real things instead of forever juggling words... Might start by washing this window, it's filthy."

He was wearing short pants and a white t-shirt. Should he change? What for? He poked his head into the music room. "Shizuko, I'm going out for a bit. Be home for dinner."

She gave a barely perceptible nod and went on with her playing.

———

It is good, thought Hiranuma, sitting with closed eyes on the Sapporo-bound train, to have a lifelong friend. Everyone should have one, and yet how many people do?

He and Sawamoto had known each other since nursery school. Through elementary school, high school and college they had been inseparable, closer than twin brothers. They had double-dated, Hiranuma squiring Shizuko, Sawamoto this girl or that – he was pleasing but not easily pleased, and never remained with the same girl for long. Three times married, twice divorced and once widowed, now living with a woman half his age, Sawamoto could definitely claim the more exciting life of the two. Which was fine with

Hiranuma. Excitement was not something he craved. Excitement he could live without; the world would be the better for a little less of it.

At the station he'd mechanically purchased a newspaper, and now, jolted out of his reverie by a high school girl flinging herself with superfluous energy into the seat beside him, he scanned the headlines. Another cabinet minister resigning over campaign funding irregularities; another terrorist suicide bombing in the Middle East; another climatologist presenting fresh evidence that the earth was warming, the ozone layer thinning, polar ice melting and seas rising even faster than had been supposed. This girl beside him, now – did she read the papers? What effect would all this grim news have on someone her age? He felt an unaccountable impulse to engage her in conversation, to ask her... but it wouldn't do; she would immediately think he wanted to molest her, and besides, so absorbed was she in her cell phone – what sort of messages would that hyperactive thumb of hers be tapping out? and to whom? – that anyone in her vicinity, looking at her, might well come to doubt his own existence, and that of the world as well.

The Cinnamon and Clover was at Kotoni Station. Hiranuma folded his newspaper and cleared his throat. Without for an instant breaking the rhythm of her tapping, the girl swung her legs over just enough to allow him to pass. As he did so he saw her face. She was rather homely, poor child – lusterless hair, thick glasses, flat nose. A strange sensation came over him. He did not at once know how to interpret it. It was a kind of pity, an aching, stabbing pity – but for whom? For this girl? Because she was homely? No, her homeliness was beside the point, it was something else. Was it really impossible to speak to her? Couldn't he just ask her her name? No, out of the question. If he had been a fly, or a speck of dust, or gazing at her from a prison in another dimension, she could not have been less aware of his presence than she was as he hovered over her, evidently with something on his mind. You'd think she'd have been curious at least, or alarmed... but no, her detachment was supreme; her tapping went on uninterrupted.

"Well," grunted Sawamoto. "Sit down. Ono-kun!" – that to a young waiter who, hearing his name called, came striding over. "My friend here has a bit of catching up to do. What'll it be?"

"Oh...scotch."

"Make it a double. And another shochu for me. Listen," he said as soon as the waiter had left, "what do you say to you and me taking a little trip?"

"A trip? Where?"

"I don't know. India?"

"India! What would we do in India?"

Sawamoto laughed. "Bathe in the Ganges, what else? What's the news from Zenibako?"

"The news from Zenibako... Do you know what I was doing when you called? Trying to write an essay on Akutagawa."

"Ah, Akutagawa." A vague, dreamy smile softened the contours of Sawamoto's face. Amazing, thought Hiranuma. It was not so much that Sawamoto looked young for his age – there was that too, of course – but that he, Hiranuma, could look at Sawamoto and see, if he chose, a six-year-old boy, or a sixteen-year-old boy, never mind that his hair, though thick, was iron-gray, and that the flesh on his ruddy face had begun noticeably to sag. "I wonder if it's the same with him when he looks at me," he thought – though he, bald except for a thin unsightly tuft just above the forehead, had no claim at all to a youthful appearance. The thought came to him, as it did almost every time he met Sawamoto and looked with envy at his trim, muscular body, that he really should try to get in shape a bit. He had let himself go to an unpardonable degree. And yet as boys he, Hiranuma, had been far the more athletic of the two, a consistent medal-winner on Track and Field Day and a splendid mid-fielder on the Zenibako Junior High School soccer team.

"Ah, Akutagawa," sighed Sawamoto. "Do you remember what he meant to us?"

"Remember! How can I forget? We discovered him at thirteen, and it was love at first sight. Hero-worship, anyway. Hero-worship at first sight. Reading him, we made up our minds to become writers."

"And you actually did become one."

"Don't make me laugh."

"What's the matter with you?"

They fell silent as the waiter returned with their drinks, and the silence lengthened as Hiranuma, eyes closed, savored the first sip of scotch.

"What do you mean, 'don't make me laugh,'?" asked Sawamoto after a time.

"Eh? What were we talking about? Hm. Excellent scotch. But actually you can't judge by a first sip. The first sip of almost any scotch is marvelous. The real test is the second sip, or the third."

"We were talking about Akutagawa."

"Yes. He died eighty years ago this year, and Chuo Koron asked me to write a commemorative essay. Which, as you can imagine, I was only too happy to do. But then I started rereading his stories and... have you read him lately?"

"Well, I teach Rashomon every year. Never seem to grow tired of it."

"What about the kids?"

"Oh, the kids! They, of course, have more important things on their minds. Literature to them is... how shall I say this, now?... not what it was to us."

"No."

"Well? You were rereading the stories... and?"

"And... I don't know. Maybe it's me. We admired them so much, and now..."

"They don't stand the test of time?"

23

"Rashomon, granted, is in a class by itself. But the others... beyond a certain facile cleverness, I seem to see very little in them. Maybe it's just... hm... maybe it's a phase I'm going through."

Sawamoto laughed heartily, and Hiranuma smiled. "It's just a phase you're going through" had been a favorite saying of Sawamoto's older sister, who had once looked down at her teenage brother and his friends from the great height of her new-fledged adulthood. "And how is Yoshie these days?" Hiranuma asked.

"Fine, fine. Her older boy is getting married next month."

———————

"Let's go somewhere for dinner," said Sawamoto.

Hiranuma shook his head. "I can't. I promised Shizuko I'd be back. What time is it?" He looked at his watch. "Good heavens! After five already. I'd better – "

"Sit, sit! What's the matter with you? You've been married thirty years. High time you demanded a longer leash!"

"Leash?"

"Don't mind me, I'm drunk. At least stay for one more round. Ono-kun!"

"No, really, I – "

"Call her, tell her you'll be an hour late! If domestic happiness comes at the price of not being permitted to have dinner with an old friend once in a blue moon – "

"It's not that, it's…"

"It's what?"

"I don't know, she's…"

"Is anything wrong?"

Hiranuma sighed. "Not wrong exactly... Well.... The other day... it was strange..."

"Another round," said Sawamoto to the waiter, who bowed slightly and vanished. "Well?" he prompted Hiranuma. "What was strange?"

"You know that narrow little road that skirts the beach, out by the – "

"My dear child. My dear boy. I grew up in Zenibako, remember? There's no need for you to walk me through the place. I can close my eyes and see it as clearly as you see it when you're there. Yes, I know the narrow little road that skirts the beach. Know every bend, every rise and fall in it. Every pothole. What about it?"

"On both sides of the road there are hamanasu bushes."

"When the book royalties dry up you can become a tour guide. Don't you remember? Our mothers used to go out there together to pick hamanasu. They boiled it down to make hamanasu jam, which I hated because it tasted just like boiled tomatoes."

"Well, Shizuko went out there on her bike the other day... What's today?"

"Thursday."

"Monday, then. She rode out there to pick hamanasu."

"Bit early, no? Hamanasu doesn't ripen till October."

"I don't know, it's been a crazy season. Climate change, global warming, whatnot. Flowers have been blooming out of season, the cicadas began chirping in July... Anyway – oh, thank you," he said to the waiter as he laid before him another glass of scotch. "Hm... I suppose I'd better call her."

"Well, call her then."

"Is there a payphone?"

"Why don't you join the twenty-first century already and get yourself a cell phone?"

"No thank you. I'm distracted enough as it is."

"Here, use mine." Sawamoto drew it from a knapsack lying on the chair beside him and handed it over across the table.

"How do I...?"

"Just press this button and input the number. Seriously, Hiranuma. You keep resisting the new technology the way you do, and in a few years you're going to be utterly helpless."

Sawamoto sipped his shochu, closed his eyes and smiled. "Maybe I'll go to Greece instead of India," he thought. "Or Jerusalem. I've always wanted to go to Jerusalem, walk the streets trodden by the prophets of old..."

"She's not answering." Hiranuma handed the phone back to him. "She's probably still playing the piano. You can't hear the phone in there."

"Listen. Forget India. Let's go to Jerusalem."

"What?"

"Did I mention that I've been reading the Bible lately?"

"No, I don't think so."

"Yes, I.... but we'll talk about that later. I'm still waiting to hear about the strange thing that happened to Shizuko-san when she went to the narrow little road by the beach to pick hamanasu."

"Well... She comes back after an hour or so. I'm upstairs in my room wondering why Akutagawa seems so... so lifeless. Grateful for the distraction, I go downstairs to the kitchen and say how about some tea? – we usually have tea at around four-thirty... She mumbles no thanks and walks past me out of the room. A moment later I hear the door of her music room close, and she starts playing."

"How very odd!" Sawamoto exclaimed ironically, and burst out laughing. "Don't mind me, I'm drunk. Well, go on, go on!"

"Over dinner the story came out. In that narrow road she'd run into, of all people... her piano teacher."

"Her piano teacher."

"A guy in his mid-sixties. Shizuko's been his student for twenty years. I remember she once said, 'He's like a father to me.'"

"Well?"

"He was with a young girl. They were holding hands."

"Very suggestive!"

"At the sight of Shizuko... well, you can imagine his astonishment. She was about the last person he would have expected, or wanted, to meet."

"Her surprise was no less, I daresay."

"It was very... what's the word?... disconcerting. Very awkward. I can understand that, but..."

"But what?"

"She actually... I mean, you know Shizuko. Is she the sort to get all unhinged over... over something like that?"

"I wouldn't have thought so. Is she unhinged?"

"Yes! It's as if her whole world has collapsed around her! Honestly, Sawamoto, I've never, ever seen her in the state she's in!"

"Hm! But are you sure this thing with the piano teacher is the cause of it?"

"Well, she was perfectly fine up until the time she left the house on Monday afternoon, and she came back..."

"Unhinged."

"Unhinged, yes. When she speaks at all, it's about that, nothing but that – the piano teacher who was once like a father to her, How he 'lowered himself,' 'degraded himself' – those are her words. How can she ever look him in the face again? How can she ever study under him again? 'Shi-chan,' I said, 'really, you're making a mountain out of a molehill, this is his private life, it has nothing to do with you, and besides, you may be misinterpreting what you saw...' 'If you'd seen the look on his face when he saw me,' she shot back – honestly, you'd think *I* was the guilty party, the way her eyes flashed! – 'if you'd seen the look on his face, you wouldn't say I was misinterpreting! Believe me, if anything in this world is certain—'"

"Nothing is," murmured Sawamoto.

"My words exactly – and precisely the last thing I should have said! She flung past me out of the room, and the next thing I hear is the slamming of the music room door."

"Whew!"

"That was Monday night. Since then she's come round a bit, but... well, however trivial it may seem to you or me, to her, apparently, it was a great shock."

"Uncanny. Unless *she* was having an affair with him?"

Hiranuma gaped at his friend in astonishment. "Sawamoto! Did you just say what I think you said?"

"Sorry, sorry! It just slipped out!" Sawamoto was genuinely distressed. "Hiranuma, listen to me! We've known each other all our lives! You were my best friend when we were kids You're my best friend now. Shizuko-san too I've known since we were teenagers. You know I wouldn't say anything... or think anything... Damn! It's the drink. It's gone to my head! There's only one cure for that, and that's... another drink! Ono-kun!"

"No, really, I'm going."

"You're not angry?"

"No." He rose somewhat unsteadily to his feet and began fumbling in his pocket, apparently struggling to extract his wallet from a deep and tangled interior.

"My treat," said Sawamoto. "It's the least I can do, to make amends... You accept my apology?"

"Of course."

"Well, good luck at home. We'll speak again soon. Ono-kun, bring me a cup of hot strong coffee, would you? There's a good fellow!"

What time was it? He had expected the train to be full, but here was an empty seat; he fairly collapsed into it and closed his eyes. His head ached and he felt terribly disoriented. How much had he drunk? Not much, he would have thought, and yet see the effect it was having on him! "And I was hoping to get some work done tonight!"

Well, tomorrow was another day. The question was, how to recapture something of the feeling Akutagawa's writing had once awoken in him? He read and read, he strained his imagination; it was no use. When the horse is dead, you flog it in vain. Was it the horse that was dead, or he, the flogger? "Yes, maybe I'm the dead one, and Akutagawa is as alive as ever."

He must, though unaware of having done so, have fallen asleep, because all of a sudden he found himself looking out the window into the gathering darkness, wondering where on earth he was. As if in answer to his unspoken question came an unctuous recorded announcement through overhead speakers, a woman sounding like a mother welcoming her kindergarten children home: "Next stop, Zenibako, Zenibako. The doors on the left side will open."

"What! Zenibako already!" Where was everyone? The train was practically empty. He rose unsteadily to his feet, lurched heavily forward, and grabbed a strap just in time to keep from falling. The train slowed and stopped; the doors opened. Mastering his dizziness with an effort, Hiranuma strode purposefully out of the train and up the stairs into the station. He slipped his ticket into the slot and the gates opened to admit him. He scanned the milling crowd. Would Shizuko have come to meet him? He smiled at this pleasant fantasy. Yes, it really did seem for a moment as if he'd been away for a long time, months, years, and Shizuko would detach herself from the crowd and fling herself on his neck, delighted to have him home again.

Outside he was surprised at how chilly it had become – and he in short pants! What a spectacle he must present! Here was a fleet of waiting taxis – should he take one? It was tempting, but no, the night air and a brisk walk would do him good. Sure enough, no sooner had he begun to walk than he felt better. He breathed deeply. On his left was the sea, its black rippling surface glittering here and there with the reflected glow of the street lights. The waves rolled gently, producing a sound like that of leaves rustling in the breeze. How odd. He had lived here all his life; the sound of the waves was as familiar as the sound of his own breath; and yet that comparison had never occurred to him before. Which signified... what, exactly? He chuckled out loud. Yes, life was full of little surprises.

He crossed the tracks and turned right into a narrow path that led into a grove of dwarf bamboo. Only one who knew the path as well as he did could have walked it in the dark. "I wonder how many other men my age live in the house they grew up in," he mused. Yes, it was strange, though in another sense perfectly natural and ordinary. His parents had been getting on; finding the house too much to look after, they decided to sell it and move into a smaller apartment. They were delighted when Hiranuma himself had come forward as the buyer. The royalties from his first book had gone into the down payment. In a sense he was still living off that first book of his. His reputation, such as it was, rested on it. For a time it had been a bestseller and was selling even now, a quarter of a century later. "Yes," he thought, chuckling again, "I peaked before I was thirty, and it's been downhill ever since!"

He came out of the path into an unpaved lane, and turned right into another. His house was the very last one, on a bluff overlooking the sea. What was this, though – was it dark? Yes, unmistakably it was; there was not a single light on. Could Shizuko have gone to bed already?

He slipped his key into the lock and opened the door. "Shizuko?" What time was it? He had the distinct impression of having left the bar before six, but an after-midnight feeling pervaded the house – and not only the house; hadn't the train been strangely empty? Well, there was no accounting for the things that can happen when you're drinking – still, he hadn't drunk *that* much... At least he didn't think he had. In the hallway he stumbled against something and lurched forward, but managed to keep from falling, and in the kitchen he switched on the light. The clock on the wall above the sink settled the question of time: it was ten minutes past eight, about what he would have figured. So there was no time warp, no hours lost to a drunken stupor; true, he was just the slightest bit giddy, and would hesitate to trust himself behind the wheel of a car, but otherwise he was sober enough; he could rely on his sensory apparatus to more or less tell him the truth about the world; or if not that at least about his immediate surroundings.

"Shizuko!" he called out, slightly louder this time. He saw no sign of any dinner preparations under way. Could she be still in the music room? Sitting on her piano stool, staring vacantly into the darkness and brooding about the piano teacher and his young paramour, or whatever she was? Really, this was too much. He, Hiranuma, was by no means a forceful personality; there was nothing of the authoritarian in him; still, wasn't it time to tell Shizuko in no uncertain terms that enough was enough, that whatever her own views on the question of marital fidelity, this was not a matter that concerned her and she was to put it out of her mind once and for all? "If you really feel so strongly about it, get yourself another piano teacher, but this endless brooding – it simply won't do!"

Yes, that is what he would tell her. He should have taken a firm line sooner. Sometimes a woman needs that – not only a woman; all of us. We come to a crisis in our life, real or imagined, and risk magnifying it out of all proportion without someone – husband, wife, father, mother, teacher – to give us a little shake and say, "Enough! Time to move on, get on with your life!"

He proceeded along the dark corridor to the music room, his certainty that she was there diminishing with every step he took. At the door he paused. "She won't be there, and then what'll I do?" A kind of despair came over him. It froze him; he had never felt anything quite like it before. "What is this? What's going on?" He flung open the door. The curtains had not been drawn; the room was bathed in pale moonlight. The piano, a baby grand, was open, and sheet music rested on the stand.

"Should I call the police?" he thought, closing the door behind him. A scene unfolded in his mind: siren blaring, a police car screeches to a halt in front of the house; the officer gets out of the car and he, Hiranuma, struggling to make himself heard above the wail of the siren, explains the situation. "Have you checked the bedroom?" asks the officer, at which Hiranuma, blushing and stammering, admits that the idea simply hadn't entered his head.

———————

Yes, there she was, curled up in her futon, under the goose down quilt he had bought her for her birthday three years ago. Born in the south of Japan, she had come to Hokkaido at fourteen, her father having been transferred by his company to its Sapporo office. You'd think she would long ago have got used to the cold, but she never had; even now the Hokkaido winter was too much for her.

"Shizuko?"

She did not stir.

"Well, let her sleep," he thought. He turned to go, but paused in the doorway. Retracing his steps, he approached the foot of the futon. Looking down at her, he was struck by a youthful, almost childlike quality in her face. She was probably dreaming about her childhood; she often did. "Don't you?" she'd asked him once, and was surprised when he replied, "No, never." "And yet," she said, smiling, "you live in the house you grew up in!"

"I'll have a bath, fix myself a bite of dinner, then go upstairs and try to get some work done." But the segment of his brain that made decisions and the segment that generated physical movement seemed to have parted company. He continued to stand there, gazing at his wife's face.

What was it about that face that set her apart from all other women in the world? They had met in (of all places!) a university physics class. He was majoring in literature, she in music. In those days arts students needed at least one science credit in order to graduate. Charming coincidences lubricated their early friendship: each had originally selected biology and been turned away because the course was full; both had blundered into physics as a last resort; they soon fell hopelessly behind, and took comfort in each other, shyly and hesitantly at first, gradually more openly. Shizuko was not only Hiranuma's first love; she was his first female friend, the first girl with whom he'd had even a casual relationship – the first girl, in a word, whose mere presence had not terrified him into a state of shrinking imbecility.

He loved her. He who had never loved before fell in love with her face before he'd ever heard her voice; then he fell in love with her voice, with the words her voice uttered, with the slightly crooked teeth she exposed when she smiled, with the tiny cluster of freckles on her forehead that reminded him of stars – in short, with every feature and quality she possessed, not because those features and qualities were demonstrably good in themselves, but because they were hers. That is how a shy teenage boy loves, and there is nothing surprising about it; what is perhaps surprising is that he loved her the same way now, at fifty-four.

II

"God is not dead!" Sawamoto declaimed.

"No, of course not," said young Ono, the waiter, gravely. "Let me call you a taxi."

"He's not dead. He simply said, 'Ok, children, you're grown up now, you're on your own'…"

"Sir, really, it's almost closing time. Let me call you a taxi."

"…and He left! 'I've fulfilled my responsibilities,' He said – 'created the world, created mankind, nurtured him when he was helpless…' But infancy doesn't last forever! It's too bad, it would be better if it did, far better if it did – don't you think so, Ono? If you had a choice now – wouldn't you choose to be an infant forever? I know I would. Hm. A taxi, you say. No, I don't think so. I think I'll take a walk. How much do I owe?"

"Twenty-two thousand three hundred yen."

"No! Really? Did I drink as much as that?"

"You and your friend."

"Ah, my friend! Of course. I'd forgotten. My friend. I'll tell you a little secret, Ono, which you're too young to have discovered on your own. We have no friends. When all is said and done, we are alone. No God, no friends… Tell me something. Supposing I were to say to you, 'I left my wallet at home, I can't pay.' Would you let me go, trusting me to come back tomorrow? Or would you call the police?"

"I'd have to ask the manager."

"Let me tell you a little story. Bear with me for just one more minute. When I was a student I had a part-time job at a little bar very much like this one. One day an elderly gentleman very much like I am now – urbane, distinguished, erudite, but with an unfortunate tendency to drink too much and, when he did, to talk too much – one day this elderly gentleman said to me, 'I left my wallet at home. I can't pay.' And without the slightest hesitation, without asking the manager, I said to him, 'That's all right, sir, you'll pay next time.' I believe his bill too came to twenty-two thousand... what was it?"

"Twenty-two thousand three hundred."

"Quite so. Twenty-two thousand three hundred. Well, you'll think about what I've told you, Ono, won't you? Twenty...two...thousand... here's twenty-five. Keep the change. A little tip. Something to remember me by."

"Won't you be coming again, sir?"

"Probably not for some time. I've been thinking, you see, of taking a little trip. Well, goodbye. All the best."

He was free at last. As he opened the door and breathed in the night air, it really did seem to him as though young Ono had been holding him against his will in that oppressive air infused with alcohol fumes and cigarette smoke – that he had endured it all that time only for Ono's sake. "What's this?" he thought; "rain?" Yes, a faint drizzle was falling; you couldn't feel individual drops, but before you knew it your face was wet, your clothes damp and clinging, your glasses misted over until the lights of this dull, featureless little suburb looked like a scene from a Monet painting. "Maybe I'll go to Paris..."

He walked with a long purposeful stride, but without any idea of where he was going. He came to a red light and stopped; then, laughing at himself, he crossed in defiance of the light. "Pavlov's dogs, that's what we are. Pavlov's dogs. Not a car in sight, but the light is red, and the good citizen stops! Since when have I become such a good citizen? I let down my guard for an instant, and behold – Sawamoto Toshiaki, good citizen!

"What a fool I am." He had called Hiranuma intending to confer with him about a certain matter, and instead their talk had meandered into this channel and that, and suddenly Hiranuma was on his way, the matter on Sawamoto's mind unaddressed, not so much as mentioned. "What if I call him again, now?" What time was it? He glanced at his watch – "What! After eleven already!" He should be getting home; Kaori would be waiting up for him. "Poor Kaori," he thought. Such beauty as she possessed he had never, ever encountered in a woman – never; not in person, not in a movie, not in the paintings of even the greatest masters. Once upon a time she'd been his student. True, the admission standards at the women's college he taught at were less than rigorous; still, it was something of a mystery to him how she had managed to meet them. She was not retarded, at least not in the clinical sense, but painfully, painfully slow all the same, and the blank incomprehension with which she faced every situation that confronted her would have made life on her own impossible – at least so Sawamoto would have thought. Her helplessness had melted his heart. Was it part of her beauty? Perhaps it was. He newly divorced and she newly graduated, they had drifted together, becoming first lovers, then roommates – or whatever their living arrangement could be called. Two years had passed since then, and still that imbecile beauty of hers fascinated him. Hiranuma was a writer; maybe he could make something of it – if he ever saw her, that is. Sawamoto had never introduced them, had only spoken of her in the vaguest terms, and Hiranuma for his part had never shown any curiosity. Hiranuma and that Shizuko of his. Homely though she was, she was the only woman he saw, the only woman he had ever seen. When it came to matters sexual, Hiranuma and Sawamoto were polar opposites; neither understood the other, and each regarded the other with a kind of pitying contempt.

"Yes, I'd better be heading home," he thought again. "Well, all right then, home. Where's the station? No, really..." He slipped his knapsack off his back and rummaged about in it in the dark, finding at last what he was looking for – his cell phone. "Why doesn't Hiranuma have a cell phone like everyone else?" Calling him on his home phone at this hour would be awkward. "Am I drunk enough to shrug that off? If I can pose the question, probably not. So the solution is to get a little drunker. But where? All the bars around here are closed. I'd have to go to Susukino or something. Excuse me" – this to a passerby under an umbrella. "Which way's the station?"

"Straight ahead two blocks, then turn right."

"Ah."

Whether he went to Susukino or went home, the station was his first stop. Come to think of it, hadn't Kaori warned him as he left the house that morning to take his umbrella? The sun had been shining then, and the weather forecast said nothing about rain, but shouldn't he know by now that Kaori, stupid though she was when it came to rational thinking, possessed certain instincts that never played her false? It was not that she had a peculiar gift for weather forecasting – she had a peculiar gift for forecasting, period. She was a seer, a prophetess, a Cassandra – and he, true to form, had not believed her, with the result that now he was getting soaked to the skin. He never learned. Maybe *he* was the stupid one. It's people who think they're intelligent, who take their intelligence for granted – they're the ones most easily led astray. Yes, once upon a time he and Hiranuma had been the two smartest kids in Zenibako, maybe in all Hokkaido. Hiranuma at least had a handful of books to show for it – not great books, rather far from it, but books all the same. As for himself, what was he? A teacher of miscellaneous literature (the polite term was "comparative" literature) in an insignificant

41

college, repository for kids who couldn't get into better places. Soon he wouldn't even be that.

"Home," he decided as he approached the station.

"Would you like some hot tea?" Kaori asked as she helped him off with his knapsack.

"Yes," said Sawamoto, "because it's you who offer it, and only for that reason. Why aren't you in bed?"

"I'm not sleepy."

"What were you doing?"

"Reading."

"Reading what?"

"Moby-Dick."

It was the only book she ever read. "You must know it by heart by now. Go ahead. Recite it. Let's see how far you get."

"Have a bath first. I'll get your tea ready."

"Recite Moby-Dick."

"'Call me Ishmael. Some years ago – never mind how long precisely – having little or no money in my purse, and nothing particular to interest me on shore'..."

"You know, maybe that's what I'll do! Take a cue from old Ishmael and 'see the watery part of the world'. What do you think, Kaori-chan – shall we go a-whaling?"

"Oh, let's!"

"We'll sleep on it, and see how we feel in the morning. How many women, by the way, were there on the Pequod? Do you happen to remember?"

"None."

"It's no place for you, Kaori. Well, I'll have a bath."

"Go. The water is hot. You're wet. I told you to take your umbrella, didn't I?"

"You did. Next time you tell me to do something, I swear I'll listen."

"No you won't. I'm Cassandra, under Apollo's curse. I have the gift of prophecy, but no one believes me."

"I'll believe you."

"Who sees the future better, you or me?"

"You."

"Well, what I see is that you won't believe me. Go."

———

"There have been cultures in this world where they sacrificed women like her," he mused to himself as the hot water lapped his chin. He closed his eyes. "How strange," he thought. "When I was a kid I used to wonder what sin I'd committed that merited the punishment of being Sawamoto Toshiaki. It could only have been something dire, something horrible, something beyond a boy's imagination. I wanted to grow up fast. Maybe as a grownup I'd know what I had done. Alas, no. I grew up in vain. At college I studied foreign cultures, foreign languages – why? To escape my own background; to escape being *me*. It's funny – not even to Hiranuma did I ever breathe a word of this, and yet he must have guessed – *intuited*, I suppose the word would be – since the main character in his second novel is clearly based on me, and he suffers from that very complaint – *illness*, I really should call it. Maybe Hiranuma himself suffered from it. Maybe everyone does. A pity, a genuine pity, that Hiranuma isn't a better writer. Not that he doesn't have talent of a kind; but to tackle a theme like that you need genius. Never mind. He's done all right for himself. He has a past, a present, even a future – while all I have is this hot water lapping against my chin – and enough self-pity to choke a horse." He smiled. "Ah, yes! Well, enough. Kaori is waiting with tea."

———

"Why are you wasting your youth with me?" Sawamoto said. "Get yourself a boyfriend your own age; marry; have children. Live! Ah, Kaori-chan, of the many, many sins for which I will have to render account to my Maker, the worst, positively the worst, will be robbing you of your youth."

"Are you tired of me?"

"The day I'm tired of you will be the day I'm tired of life, and there'll be only one thing left to do, and that's put a bullet through my brain. You misunderstand me. Don't you want a home, a child?"

"I have a home – right here. And I have a child – you." She giggled, raising a hand to her mouth in girlish embarrassment. "You're my child, and I'm your mother."

"There's some truth in that," Sawamoto agreed.

"More tea?"

"No, I don't think so. Listen. I'm going to tell you a secret. You're not to tell anybody. Okay? Can you keep a secret?"

"Yes. Tell me."

"All right then. The people at Wakaba Women's College – the people in the office, the people who make the decisions – "

"Mr. Ozawa?"

"Yes, him and the others on the steering committee. They want me to take early retirement. They want to phase me out. Me and my subject. They have to cut costs, you see, and comparative lit doesn't pay."

"Doesn't pay! You taught me everything I know!"

Smiling, Sawamoto reached out and laid his hand on hers. He stroked her long, delicate fingers "That's not enough, apparently. It's a fact, you know, that these days literature is not high on people's lists of subjects you need to master in order to get ahead in the world. Commerce, science, engineering – that's where the action is. Literature is at best an adornment, not a serious pursuit. One lit prof is enough, they've decided, and Professor Kaga, being younger, better-looking and also a bit of a celebrity, having

45

appeared on TV, is their preference. The retirement package they've offered me is very generous. It would settle us pretty comfortably for years to come."

"What did you tell them?"

"I haven't given them an answer yet. Ozawa has given me a week to think it over. This evening I met up with my old friend Hiranuma – you've heard me speak of him – intending to ask his advice, but somehow the subject never came up."

"Don't take it."

"No?"

"Spit in their faces and walk out. Don't take it."

Sawamoto laughed out loud. "My dear, that's very nice, very theatrical, it'll make for a lovely effect, but what'll I do with myself?"

"You can get another job, at another school."

"At my age? I'm fifty-four, Kaori-chan. Schools don't hire fifty-four-year-old rejects from other schools."

"Well, persuade them to change their minds. You can do it. You can persuade anyone to do anything."

III

Hiranuma woke with a start, bathed in sweat. At first he didn't know where he was, or who he was. Slowly the sound of Shizuko's rhythmic breathing steadied him. He closed his eyes and lay back on the pillow. "What a frightful dream!" What time was it? It was pitch dark. In the dream he'd had an invisible, soundless gun. His rampage had begun with Shizuko. Then he went out and killed old Iihara-san as he pruned the azalea shrubs in his garden. His next victim was an old woman walking her dog. The dog was a big coal-black animal. It sprang for Hiranuma's throat but, barely off the ground, dropped like a stone. Hiranuma's aim was unerring. He strolled through the unpaved lanes and paved streets of Zenibako, killing everyone he met – people he knew, people he didn't know. Sirens wailed in vain. He killed and killed, his pleasure mounting to an almost unbearable pitch. Yes, this was power, this was freedom! To kill and kill and kill, pointlessly, purposelessly, and yet not to be so much as suspected!

"My God!" he thought. "How could I dream something so... monstrous? What does it mean?" He peered through the darkness at Shizuko lying beside him. Such peaceful sleep! Did nothing, nothing of his agitation communicate itself to her?

Careful not to wake her, he eased himself slowly out of his futon. "I'd better have a bath, I'm all sweaty. No, I'll have a cup of hot milk."

He switched on the light in the kitchen and saw it was ten past four. "Almost morning." And yet still dark. Yes, the nights were getting longer. Soon autumn would begin in earnest. He took a carton of milk from the fridge, measured out a cupful, poured it into a pot and put it on the stove.

He sank into a chair and closed his eyes. "My God."

"Good morning."

Hiranuma gasped. Shizuko stood smiling in the doorway, rubbing her eyes. "I took a pill and slept like a corpse. What time did you get home? What are you making? Hot milk? What time is it?"

"Would you like some?"

"It's the middle of the night!"

"Well, go back to sleep."

"No, I've slept enough. More than enough. Where were you last night? I have a vague recollection of you going out."

"I had a drink with Sawamoto. I came home for supper, as I said I would, but you were already asleep."

"I'm sorry. I haven't been – your milk's boiling!"

Hiranuma sprang to his feet, managing to turn off the fire just in time to prevent the milk from boiling over. He poured the frothy liquid into his cup and sat down again. "Haven't been what?"

"Haven't been... myself. Youth doesn't last forever, you know."

"What do you mean by that?"

"I believe the technical term is menopause."

"No! Really?"

"Will you still love me when I'm an old lady?"

"I'll love you as long as you're you."

"Yes, but when I'm an old lady will I be me?"

"I had a dreadful dream last night." He told her, omitting the detail that she had been his first victim. She sensed the gap in the narrative.

"What about me?" she asked. "Did I survive the rampage?"

"No, dear. You didn't."

"Don't look so... There is a difference, you know, between killing someone and *dreaming* you killed someone. Besides – is there a better way to go?"

"What do you mean?"

"It's the perfect death. The very opposite of the slow deterioration and lingering agony that's more likely in store for us."

"Shizuko! What are you saying – that you want to die?"

"Let's reason this out. Supposing you had a choice. Supposing a god appears to you. 'Hiranuma-san,' he says, 'you are a good man – not a perfect man, not the best of men, but a good man all the same, and your reward is this choice which I am now offering you: you can die right now, right this minute, peacefully, painlessly, or you can go on living to a ripe old age and die of cancer, your brain eaten away by Alzheimer's...' What would you choose?"

"I... I don't know."

"Don't you ever think about it?"

"Yes, but..."

"For me, the choice would be easy. 'Take me now,' I'd say."

———————

49

After a bath, Hiranuma got dressed and climbed the stairs to his office. The day had got off to an unusually early start; even now it was only twenty minutes to eight. The sky was a cloudless pale blue. It was a September sky but an August sun, glaring, intense, malevolent, and the thermometer on the wall next to a photograph he wouldn't part with for all the money in the world showed twenty-six degrees. He slid open the window. Shizuko's garden, in which she grew all manner of vegetables, was blocked from view by the red vinyl roof, stained here and there with bird droppings, of the house's first floor. Dragonflies flitted through the air. Beyond the roof, past a row of scraggly trees whose leaves here and there already showed traces of yellow, was the sea, Ishikari Bay. "How strange," he thought; "I live right on the sea and yet I neither fish nor swim." He had done both as a boy, and no doubt could now if he wanted to... "But let's see if I can get some work done."

He sat down at his desk and switched on his laptop. Sawamoto made fun of him for "not joining the 21st century." True, he frowned on cell phones, but he had taken to computers readily enough, and did all his work on one. "Supposing there had been computers in Akutagawa's day," he thought lazily. "Would his stories have turned out differently?"

He called up the essay he'd been writing, and frowned. "Is this all I've done?" He read it over, his frown deepening with every word. "Have I sunk to this?" Even as a rough draft it seemed to reflect badly on him. There was only one thing to do – delete and start again. Or... better still, call Chuo Koron and say he was sorry, he just didn't have the essay in him, and rather than submit something unworthy either of the master or of himself, he preferred to bow out while there was still time. "But that's the trouble – there *isn't* still time, they're expecting it by early next week. I've committed myself, I must soldier on, praying to the gods for some spark of inspiration, some glimmer of insight, some... *something*.. If only it wasn't so hot! It's September, September!"

He stood up, his disgust at the weather merging with his disgust at himself. "If that god of Shizuko's came to me now, right this minute, with his proposition, I think... I think I'd know what to say." Absent-mindedly he moved over to the window. The lone photograph thumbtacked just next to it, badly faded, showed a child of three in a white dress and a funny little white sun bonnet. It was Shizuko. She had given it to him when they were teenagers. Quite possibly she had forgotten its existence; she never came up to the second floor, never entered his office – not that he had forbidden her to, he certainly had nothing to hide. What if she did come up and saw it there – would she be surprised?

Returning to his desk, he picked up a book lying on it, one of several, a collection of Akutagawa stories. Idly he flipped through the pages; then, when nothing in particular caught his eye, he turned with a sort of grim purposefulness to the table of contents. He would pick a story and force himself to read it through, if force was the only thing that worked. Surely, if he chose his story wisely, something of his former admiration for the author would come to life again; even if it meant having to write about his past feelings as though they were present, he should be able to grind out *something*; he was an experienced writer, after all, and they weren't asking him for a book, just two thousand words at most; fifteen hundred would do... Really, what was the matter with him? Shizuko had mentioned menopause; maybe something of the sort was affecting him too.

Here was one that looked promising: Autumn Mountain. Yes, yes... A memory, vague at first, slowly took shape, of him and Sawamoto – how old would they have been? thirteen? fourteen? – each perched on a separate rock at the beach, watching the waves roll in, and he, Hiranuma, urging Sawamoto to read that particular story; he himself had just read it the night before and... He blushed as an expression he'd used came back to him: "All of life is contained in those four pages!" The ironic smile that was so characteristic of Sawamoto had come to him somewhat later in life. At that time, at fourteen, he had not had it; no, then he had unabashedly shared his friend's boyish enthusiasm. The two boys immediately ran back to Hiranuma's house. Hiranuma handed him the book and waited patiently, scarcely daring to breathe lest he distract Sawamoto's concentration while Sawamoto, sitting cross-legged on the floor, read, to all appearances perfectly oblivious to everything going on in the world outside the story.

"'And speaking of Ta Ch'ih, have you ever seen his Autumn Mountain painting?'

"'No, I haven't seen it. And you?'

"'Well, strange to say, I'm not really sure whether or not I have seen it...'"

That is the perplexing dialogue with which the story begins. Two elderly connoisseurs of painting are sipping tea and discussing the great thirteenth-century master Ta Ch'ih. Having piqued his host's curiosity, the guest then proceeds to tell his story. ("Yes, it's coming back to me," murmured Hiranuma to himself.) The story's structure is vintage Akutagawa: something heard by one character is transmitted to another and then to a third, so that by the time it gets to the reader it has been mutilated by distortion, willful exaggeration and lapses of memory. Many years ago a certain art critic heard a rumor of a lost Ta Ch'ih masterpiece owned by a collector in a distant province. He makes the journey, introduces himself to the collector, and is shown the painting. It is beautiful beyond his wildest dreams. How does one describe beauty? Beauty is indescribable, but few writers, Hiranuma had to admit, could better evoke it than Akutagawa. "The mountain and its hills were fresh green, as if newly washed by rain..."But it was not so much the description of the painting as Akutagawa's account of its effect on the viewer that transformed what otherwise would have been, to Hiranuma, mere scenery into something majestic, something to make the heart throb. Yes, his heart was throbbing now.

The visiting critic's attempts to persuade the owner to sell him the painting are in vain. He returns home, defeated and yet uplifted. He doesn't *own* the painting, true, and may never set eyes on it again, but he has seen it, hasn't he? And having seen it, he will surely not forget it. It will infuse his life, *beautify* his life. Decades pass. The connoisseur who is narrating the story now comes to the point, which is his own attempt, having heard of the older critic's discovery of the painting, to see Autumn Mountain for himself. He makes his own journey to the distant province. The original owner is long dead and his collection dispersed, but inquiries lead him to a certain nobleman said to have inherited Autumn Mountain. The nobleman ushers his visitor inside; yes, certainly, it will be his delight and his pleasure to show the painting to his honored guest; he orders it brought out of storage and hung on the wall; there it is... yes, yes, it is beautiful, marvelous, perfect – "And yet... and yet I felt at once that this was not the same painting that Yen-k'o had seen once long ago. No, no, a magnificent painting it surely was, yet just as surely not the unique painting which he had described with such religious awe!"

Hiranuma closed the book. For a time his mind seemed to go blank; then he noticed that he was breathing more rapidly than usual, as though after an unaccustomed physical exertion. The sound of waves reached him through the open window. He turned to see a huge swarm of dragonflies flying past. "How many would there be there?" he wondered idly. "Thousands, millions..." There seemed no end to them.

"I wonder if Sawamoto remembers," he thought. "Hm. What would he be doing now? Maybe I'll call him and ask him. Should I? What time is it?"

9:12, said the lower right-hand corner of his computer screen. Hastily, without even glancing at them, he deleted the few paragraphs he'd written. "Would he be teaching now? He'll be surprised to hear from me, I hardly ever call him, it's always he who calls me, for some reason..." Yes, it was true; that had never struck him before. "Well, I'll dial his number."

He walked slowly, as though seeking to avoid notice, down the stairs. At the sight of Shizuko in the hallway he gave a slight start: "Oh!"

"What's the matter?"

"Nothing. I just... I thought I'd give Sawamoto a call..."

"Sawamoto?"

"Yes, I want to ask him something... about Akutagawa. I'm working on a piece about Akutagawa, you see, and..."

"Come into the kitchen with me. I have something to tell you."

He looked at her in quizzical bewilderment, surprised at her sudden firmness of purpose, but she did not meet his eyes. She turned abruptly and proceeded into the kitchen, leaving him to follow. She was seated at the table before he entered the room.

"Sit down."

"What is it? What's the matter?" There are horrors in life; he was acutely aware of having been spared them so far; what was Shizuko about to hit him with? Had his turn come at last?

"Sit."

"All right. What is it?"

"Once, a very long time ago, before we were married, Sawamoto and I... Sawamoto and I... slept together."

She paused, looking at him intently. Hiranuma's eyes were fixed on her, but he saw nothing. His mind was blank. The only thought of which he was conscious was a palpably stupid one. It was: "I wonder what my face looks like at this moment."

The silence lengthened. He became aware of the sound of the refrigerator motor, and thought, "We've had that fridge for over a quarter of a century."

"I wanted you to know," she said at last. "I thought you should. It's been weighing on me."

"Why?" he said in a strangled voice.

"I'm not sure. Was I wrong? Should I have kept the secret? Kept you in the dark?"

"Kept me in the dark! Shizuko, I've been 'in the dark' for thirty... for thirty years." With despair and disgust he heard the trembling, the quivering in his voice; it was a mouse's voice, not a man's; it positively squeaked. "Why now? Why all of a sudden?"

"When I saw Nakagawa-sensei with that... that woman..."

"Well? What? What does Nakagawa-sensei have to do with it?"

"The revulsion, the revulsion I felt, the loathing... it was not really of him, but of me, of me, for what I did with... with Sawamoto.... It brought it all back, made me... made me... relive it... I'm sorry, I shouldn't have... I just... I just *had* to!"

"Had to what?"

"Had to tell you."

"I see. And now that you've told me, what... what...?"

Sobbing helplessly, Shizuko was unable to answer. She only shook her head back and forth, as though vigorously denying something.

———————

When the fog in his brain lifted, he couldn't recall having returned to his office; nor did he know how long he had been standing at the window, watching the dragonflies – for it was they that seemed to be engaging his attention. The sun was hotter and brighter than ever. This was beyond even August heat; probably some sort of meteorological record was being set; he would read about it in the paper tomorrow. Climate change, global warming... in a few decades his beloved Zenibako would be tropical; if he chanced to return to it in some future life he would not recognize it. From the sun's position in the sky he judged it to be about mid-morning – ten, ten-thirty. He strained his ears. Was Shizuko playing? No, there was not a sound to be heard anywhere – except, now that the notion of sound had come into his head, that of a train going by – to Sapporo, or to Otaru? You'd think it would be obvious, from the sound, but it didn't seem to be; maybe his ears were just not sensitive enough. Shizuko, with her musician's ears, would surely know.

Shizuko. What was she doing? Still crying? Yes, he had left her in tears, he remembered now. Should he go down and comfort her? Tell her it didn't matter? It didn't, of course. Something that happened thirty years ago with no consequences at the time doesn't start mattering now. They'd been kids – not living, just playing at life. They weren't married, she didn't owe him a wife's fidelity, no one was in the wrong, no crime had been committed... "Look," he would say to her – he sat down at the desk as he began mentally composing his speech – "what you've told me changes nothing, nothing. I love you, Sawamoto is my best friend... In fact, I still want to call him, I want to ask him about this Akutagawa story I just read. We read it together when we were kids. In fact, why don't you read it, it's a wonderful story, it's called Autumn Mountain; wait, I'll get it for you..."

The words flowed through his mind, and he sat there, motionless and attentive, as though listening to someone else speak. He closed his eyes. "Really, if I'm going to write this damned essay I'd better get started. If only it wasn't so wretchedly, miserably hot! Who ever heard of such heat in September? It's crazy, idiotic!"

IV

Sawamoto, in his office at Wakaba Women's College, started at a knock on the door. Reflexively he slammed shut the book he'd been reading. Then he smiled to himself. "You'd think I'd been doing something naughty." The book was called Einstein's Universe. He'd seen it in a book store recently and purchased it on a whim. His studies had focused exclusively on literature and history; of physics, of the physical world in general, he knew nothing. The obscure thought behind his impulse to buy the book had been that it might help remedy his woeful ignorance, but it was hopeless. His reasoning power, quite adequate when put to work on familiar territory, seemed to utterly desert him here. Possibly it was the math involved; maybe "Einstein's universe" was fundamentally incomprehensible to the non-mathematical mind. Maybe he should study mathematics. It had caused him awful traumas in high school, and he had turned his back on it as soon as he got to university, but maybe now was the time.

So he had been thinking when the knock startled him out of his reverie. Tossing the book onto a pile of books on the floor behind him, he called out, "Come in." The door opened, and in stepped a young woman in black-framed spectacles.

She wore a white wool sweater, and – her glasses and shrinking shyness notwithstanding – was rather pretty. "I… I'm sorry to…" Her voice cracked and broke off. Who was she? Presumably someone in one of his classes. Could he seduce her? He seemed to love her already. What was love, after all? A feeling. What produced the feeling? It could be anything. Beauty, ugliness… What struck him now was the way her thick black hair was caught behind her shapely, tiny right ear, though the left ear was unexposed. A trivial detail, scarcely noticeable, and yet, having noticed it, he found himself unable to take his eyes off it. "Sit down," he smiled, motioning her into the chair across the desk from him. Had he ever seen her before?

"I just wanted to tell you – " her voice was a child's; if he'd been talking to her on the phone he would have guessed her age to be about twelve – "how much I… your lecture, how much I… enjoyed it…"

"Did you really? I'm so glad." What lecture would she be referring to? He had given four that day. "Please, sit down," he said again. "May I ask you what it was in particular that struck you?"

"About… about consciousness…"

Ah. That enabled him to place her in the second year comp lit class he'd taught first thing after lunch. He'd gone way off the topic on that one – something rather easy for him to do when the topic was Dickens. He had little regard for Dickens – and yet generation after generation had unanimously pronounced him a genius, "so I must be wrong," he told himself without conviction.

"I wonder..." She sat down at last. "I wonder if... I could ask you... if you're not busy..."

"No, my child."

Would she wince at "my child"? It had slipped out. No, she seemed untroubled by it.

"I wanted to... you said, I think, that... that consciousness..."

What efforts, Sawamoto wondered, had it cost her to strike up the courage to knock on the door? "Such a timid little thing!"

"What I was trying to say," he began, "was that... well, suppose we think of it this way: the brain is a physical organ. A physical, finite organ – like the stomach, for instance, or the liver, or the heart. It has its functions, and its attributes, and one of its attributes is consciousness. But what a strange, absurd notion it is – and yet how many fall prey to it! – that our consciousness, arising as it does out of a physical organ, the brain, for a physical purpose, survival, perceives *everything that exists*! Of course it doesn't! That's madness! It perceives only what it perceives, and as to what it *doesn't* perceive – why, it simply has no conception of what it doesn't perceive! No conception! No possibility of a conception. There must be whole worlds, whole *universes*..."

"Whole universes!" Her voice as she echoed him was an awed whisper.

"Whole universes – not distant from us, not light-years away, but right here, right in front of our eyes, if we had eyes to see them; at our fingertips, if we possessed the nerves to sense them... yes, whole universes, of which we know nothing and can know nothing, the greatest genius no less than the most hopeless idiot. What is beyond the range of the brain, the brain cannot know, it's as simple as that. Only the artist, perhaps, can sense something of them, these other universes – vaguely, remotely..."

"Do you believe in God?"

"In God? Do I believe in God? What do you mean – the God of the Christians?"

"Well – "

He noticed now for the first time the tiny silver cross she wore around her neck. "Are you a Christian?"

She nodded.

"Ah. Well, in that case, I have nothing to say."

"Oh, but... please..." She seemed flustered, as though fearing she had offended him in some way. "I so want... You see, I came to you because... because no one..."

"No one what, my child?"

"No one talks as you do. Listening to you, I seem to see... I don't know... I seem to glimpse... new things, new... new... new horizons..." She flushed lividly. Sawamoto regarded her in some perplexity. "She's saying, 'Take me, I'm yours,'" he thought. "You see," she went on, making an effort to master her confusion, "my parents are missionaries, they run a little church in Nakanoshima, and from the time I was an infant all I've known is God, Jesus, the Holy Mother..."

"And this no longer seems sufficient?" Sawamoto asked.

"No! My parents are like... they're like grownup children."

"And you no longer want to be a child?"

"No!"

"I see."

———————

As Hiranuma settled into his seat on the train, he noticed the girl sitting beside him and started. Was he mistaken? He must be – she could not possibly be the same one he had sat beside four days earlier on his way to meet Sawamoto, and yet... But why, on second thought, was it not possible? It was the same time of day, and no doubt most students rode the same train home from school at the same time... Still, it was a remarkable coincidence. The resemblance, or identity, was not merely in her face. Her very posture on the seat seemed identical, her very manner as she bent over her cell phone; even her hair seemed to fall about her face in exactly the same way. One could fancy her engaged in the same text-mail conversation (or whatever it was called) she'd been having the first time, typing in precisely the same words, receiving precisely the same replies.

An utterly insane thought now occurred to him. If only it were possible – but such was the unbridgeable gulf between one person and another that, innocent though the thought was, yielding to it could quite conceivably get him arrested. The idea was simply to have her read Autumn Mountain and then ask her what, if anything, it meant to her. He had the book with him, in the inner pocket of his jacket (after the brief spell of tropical heat it had suddenly turned cool enough for a jacket). How would she react if he cleared his throat or mumbled "Excuse me" or something to get her attention, and then proceeded to talk to her about the story? He could give her the book as a gift...

"Maybe it's fortunate," he thought, "that I failed to outgrow my childhood shyness. It's protecting me now from doing something totally, totally outrageous."

The pub Sawamoto had suggested they meet at this time was a place called Aphrodite, near Teine Station. Were there any bars in the city Sawamoto didn't know? Yes, he certainly got around. How dull Hiranuma was in comparison. Here was the train pulling in to Teine Station. As he stood up he made a vague effort to catch the girl's eye, but she was in another world. Would she be aware, even dimly, of his existence? Almost certainly not – but then, he reflected, why *should* she be aware of it?

He drew his jacket, a gray windbreaker, more tightly around him. It was positively chilly. Mount Teine, as he exited the station, was on the right. Every October, usually around mid-month, he and Shizuko climbed it to admire the autumn foliage. How long had that been going on? Years, decades. "A rite of passage," he thought – meaninglessly enough; the words just happened to form in his mind. Rites of passage were generally associated with spring – and, of course, with youth. "Well," he smiled, "this one is associated with autumn and age, and so much the better for it."

The Aphrodite bar was just a few paces down a narrow lane-like street lined on both sides with hole-in-corner ramen restaurants, yakitori grills, karaoke joints and neighborhood bars. It was quiet now, but at night it was probably lively enough. Hiranuma pushed open the door and squinted into the relative darkness. Sawamoto saw him first. "Hiranuma-kun!"

Sawamoto, perched on a stool at the counter, seemed the only customer in the place. "Okada-kun!" Here too, apparently, he was on familiar terms with the staff. Hiranuma settled in beside him. The bartender, a lean grizzled old man in a white apron, must have materialized from somewhere beyond Hiranuma's field of vision. He confronted Hiranuma with an air of truculent impatience, as though Hiranuma should have given his order a long time ago and was keeping him waiting unnecessarily. "Scotch," Hiranuma muttered hurriedly.

"Make it a double," said Sawamoto, precisely as he had four days before at the Cinnamon and Clover. "And another shochu for me. Listen," he said, turning on his stool to face Hiranuma. "Has the thought ever struck you – but of course it has; how could it fail to strike a thinking man? – that by the time you reach our age our life has basically been lived, and that the years remaining are, at best, redundant? At worst of course they're appalling. Of all the horrors in the world, those of old age are the most horrible. They turn life into a sick joke. I need hardly say I'm thinking of my father, whose condition in his latter years I'm sure you remember. But let's presuppose, perennial optimists that we are – eh? – let's presuppose the *best*-case scenario: you're healthy, financially secure, in full possession of your mental faculties. Even so – what's left? Travel? We've already traveled enough to know that one place is pretty much like another. Grandchildren? Neither of us has children, so that happiness, if it is one, is denied us. Love? Well, you tell me, Hiranuma. Is love at fifty-four – to say nothing of sixty-four and seventy-four – is love at fifty-four a reason for living?"

"Love?"

"Yes, love. I know how you feel about Shizuko-san and all that – ah, thank you. Kampai! We have a visiting professor of the Jewish faith with us, who tells me the Hebrew equivalent is 'l'chaim! – to life!' To life, Hiranuma, to life! What was I saying? Love. Is love at fifty-four a reason for living?"

"I don't know."

"You know, some years ago I spent a week meditating at a Zen temple. On the wall of the meditation hall there hung a sign, which said, 'Each of you must clarify the great matter of life and death. Time passes swiftly. Do not be negligent!' As for time passing swiftly, I'm sure you'll agree that it gets swifter with each passing year. Let's not be negligent, Hiranuma! Let's 'clarify the great matter of life and death.' But you're not drinking."

Hiranuma absent-mindedly sipped his scotch and said, "Do you remember a story called Autumn Mountain?"

"Autumn Mountain?"

"Akutagawa. We read it together when we were kids. Don't you remember? I – "

"Yes, yes, I think I do remember. Autumn Mountain... The image that comes to mind is of old Chinese sages... Ah! Yes! They're discussing a painting, a supremely beautiful painting, and the question it hinges on is, Does the painting actually exist?"

"Yes."

"Well?"

"Nothing. I – "

"Nothing?"

"It's just... I came across it while working on that essay, that essay I told you about, and reread it, for the first time in... Do you happen to recall how the story ends?"

"If you gave me enough time I could probably dredge it out of my memory."

"The sages are unable to determine whether the painting exists or not, but conclude that it doesn't matter, because, whether it exists or not, the image of the beautiful painting was engraved forever in their hearts. And when they realize this, they 'laughed and clapped their hands with delight.'"

"Ah. One of two things (forgive me, I'm a little drunk). Either what you've just said is utterly beside the point, or else – or else it *is* the point! Ha ha! Which is it, Hiranuma?"

"Both. Neither. I'm a little tipsy myself, I think. Does it matter whether the painting existed? Does it matter that you slept with Shizuko?"

"That I – what?"

"Slept with Shizuko."

"Hiranuma – "

"Oh, don't worry. I'm not accusing you of anything. It happened ages, ages ago, before we were married, before – "

"Hiranuma, are you mad?"

"Remember I told you about her encounter with the piano teacher and a young girl, and how strangely it affected her? Well, the key to the mystery turns out to be that the sight of them reminded her of that memory she'd suppressed all these years – "

"Hiranuma, I never slept with Shizuko."

"No?"

"Never."

"Sawamoto, you've slept with so many women, you can't be expected to remember them all."

"In another context I'd take that as a compliment. Okada-kun! Another."

"Not for me, I have to – "

"You have to nothing! Remember what we're here for!"

"What do you mean? What are we here for?"

"Why – to clarify the great matter of life and death."

"Oh, life and death need no clarifying. Life and death are clear. It's the human heart, the human heart that is muddy."

"Well, let's clarify the human heart, then. No longer ago than yesterday, Hiranuma, a girl walked into my office... a girl... I wonder if anything like this has ever happened to you..." He proceeded to tell the story, which Hiranuma, preoccupied with his own thoughts, scarcely took in.

"No, nothing like that has ever happened to me," he heard himself mumble, not sure what, if anything, he meant.

"Do you know," said Sawamoto, "there are people out there, many people, maybe even most people, who would look at our respective biographies, yours and mine, and say that you are a good man and I am a bad man. I am willing enough to credit you with being a good man, but am I bad?... I won't force you to answer if you don't want to," he smiled when Hiranuma remained silent. "I suppose your goodness extends to an unwillingness to pass judgment. How does the Bible put it? 'Judge not, that ye be not judged.' Or words to that effect. Hiranuma, you're a writer, tell me: What is 'good'? What is 'evil'? Do the words have any meaning at all?... You don't answer. You seem to have slipped into one of those 'other universes' I was talking about. Any meaning, I mean, beyond the purely conventional one – a good person obeys the rules, a bad person breaks them. And what about freedom, Hiranuma? We can't clarify the matter of life and death without considering freedom. In all the universe – this one, anyway – there is only free being: man. Every other creature – its actions are wholly determined, or very nearly so, by the laws of physics and biology. Only man is free – free to devise ends that are not rooted in physics or biology. Have you ever thought about this, Hiranuma? But of course you have. Every thinking man – "

"The other night I... I had a dream."

"Yes?"

"A dream. I dreamed I had a gun that could neither be seen nor heard. I could kill with impunity – and I did, indiscriminately, everyone I met, beginning with Shizuko. I killed and killed. Tell me: what does such a dream mean, Sawamoto?"

"It means, first of all, that you'd better have another drink. Okada-san! Tell me something, Okada-san. We were just discussing, my childhood friend here and I, whether love, past a certain age, is a reason for living. Would it be indiscreet of me to ask how old you are?"

"Eighty-one."

"Eighty-one! Really! Do you hear that, Hiranuma? Isn't it funny how a stray bit of information can alter your perspective? A moment ago I thought you looked old; now suddenly, without a wrinkle in your face having undergone the slightest alteration, you look young! But tell us, enlighten us – is love a reason for living at eighty-one?"

"I am a bartender, not a philosopher."

"Yes, I understand, but – "

"Love is no reason for living at any age. Love is a cruel trick our body chemistry plays on us to make us bring children into the world, something we'd never do in our right minds."

"Didn't Schopenhauer say that?"

"Yes, I believe he did."

"And you say you're not a philosopher! Hiramuma – let's die! I've decided. I've 'clarified the great matter.' It's time to go. Let's go together. We were practically born together, it's only fitting that we die together. Okada, you look like a man with connections – you could get us a couple of guns, couldn't you? They needn't be invisible, just ordinary ones. What do you say? We'd make it worth your while."

Deigning neither to answer nor to show any facial expression of any kind, Okada withdrew to prepare the drinks Sawamoto had ordered.

"I know what he's thinking: 'A true Japanese dies not with a gun but with a sword.' Well, he has a point, only frankly I'm terrified of pain, and I never claimed to be, or particularly wanted to be for that matter, a true Japanese. Let me tell you something about death, Hiranuma. Death is birth, and I want to be born. Well? What do you say? You ask me what your dream means. The meaning is plain – to go on encumbering the earth past your time is to wreak murderous ruin upon it."

"I don't want to die."

"No?"

"No. I want to live. You asked before if love is a reason for living at our age. My answer is yes. It is a reason for living."

"Half an hour ago you weren't so sure."

"I'm sure now."

"Really! What can have convinced you, I wonder?"

"I'm not sure. Maybe it's what you said about freedom."

"What did I say? I don't remember!"

"Well, man is free... Freedom is love... I'm not sure I... Hm. I'm a little muddled."

"Well, here, this'll take care of that," said Sawamoto as Okada, looking dour as ever, returned with their drinks.

"No, really, I've had enough, I have to – "

"Nothing of the sort! You don't order a drink and walk out leaving it undrunk! Okada-san, what do you think of a man who orders a drink and – Come, Hiranuma, one more won't kill you, and here it is, right in front of you. I won't keep you after that, I promise. I have to be going too. Kaori's waiting."

"Thank you, no." He stood up, reached into his pocket for his wallet, drew out a five thousand yen note, and slapped it on the counter. Without another word he strode, staggering just a little, towards the door.

"Hiranuma! Don't leave me here all alone!" cried Sawamoto with mock pathos. "That man," he said to Okada as soon as the door had closed behind Hiranuma, "just accused me of sleeping with his wife. Can you believe it? Of all the... I don't even *like* his wife! Phew! Ugly little thing, and a snob to boot. Thinks she's a musician. She's never heard *real* music. And Hiranuma thinks she's a treasure because he's never known a *real* woman. Ah, here comes a merry crowd. L'chaim, gentlemen, l'chaim!" he called out to a party of six gray-suited businessmen who tumbled in laughing, having evidently started their night on the town somewhere else. "Well, time for me to be off," said Sawamoto, downing his shochu in one gulp. "They're expecting me at home. Bring me the bill. How much do I owe?"

———

"Kaori, let's die."

"Yes, let's."

Sawamoto closed the apartment door behind him and let his knapsack fall to the floor. Kaori skipped up to him and they kissed. "Ugh! Shochu!" she said.

"Yes, I'm sorry. What are you cooking? It smells good."

"Of course it's good. Mackerel. Go have a bath – and brush your teeth! By the time you're through dinner will be ready."

"Never mind dinner. Get your jacket. We're going to die."

"Why do I need a jacket for that?"

"Because it's chilly out, and it's a ten-minute walk to the train station."

"Are we going somewhere?"

"We're going to jump in front of the Otaru express and be annihilated."

"All right." She disengaged herself from his embrace and went to the closet to get her jacket.

"Kaori – do you think I'm joking? I'm serious."

"Of course you are. I know."

"You know, and yet you follow me as lightly as though I'd said, 'Let's go to the supermarket to buy a few vegetables.' Recite something from Moby-Dick. Did you read today?"

"Yes."

"Recite something."

"'I, Ishmael, was one of that crew; my shouts had gone up with the rest; my oath had been welded with theirs; and stronger I shouted, and more did I hammer and clinch my oath, because of the dread in my soul. A wild, mystical, sympathetical feeling was in me; Ahab's quenchless feud seemed mine. With greedy ears – '"

"All right, that's enough. Is the bath hot?"

"Yes."

"Let's bathe together."

"We're not going to die?"

"Why would a woman like you – a girl, I should say – want to die?"

"I'm a woman. You made me a woman."

"Why would you want to die?"

"I don't want to die. Unless you do. If you do, I want to too."

"Why?"

"It's natural, isn't it?"

"No, Kaori, it's not."

"Did I do something wrong?"

"Only one thing. You attached yourself to a corrupt old man like me. You should never have done that."

"You're not a corrupt old man. You're good, and true, and I'll do everything you want me to. I'll be your slave, knowing that as your slave I'm freer than any other woman on earth."

"Come, Kaori-chan, come, child, let's have a bath."

The Miracle

"Excuse me..."

"Yes?"

"Aren't you... Yuri Kawai?"

No, I am not Yuri Kawai, though I'm mistaken for her often enough. Usually I just smile, with a half-ironic air of being sorry to disappoint, and mumble something about wishing I was. What mischievous spirit possessed me on this particular occasion? "Yes," I said. "As a matter of fact I am."

It might have had something to do with the fact – the connection is admittedly obscure – that I woke up this morning to the sound of seagulls crying and thought they were children playing. My first thought, before realizing my mistake, was, "Has summer vacation started already?"

If I'm confused, there's good reason. It suddenly turned hot – extraordinarily hot for mid-May. August heat, in a season when snow is not unheard of! It's unsettling, disorienting. And yet – such is the force of habit! – I somehow can't leave the house in the morning without putting on a sweater. It's the same with the other women at the office. We're like programmed robots, dressing by the calendar regardless of the weather.

I think I am going through a crisis in my life. I'm not sure – maybe it's nothing. There is, for example, the blind, strangling hatred I feel for that dog across the road, Kato-san's mutt. Kato-san's a widower; he lives alone. He's a taxi driver or something and works long hours. He's almost never home. What does a man like him need a dog for? Company? A mongrel like that? It doesn't bark, it doesn't howl – it *groans*. I lie awake listening to it, thinking to myself, "That's what I'd sound like if someone was torturing me." And I long to torture it in a manner worthy of those groans. I picture myself dismembering it, setting it on fire... And then I take myself to task: "It's a dog, for heaven sake! A stupid, innocent, insignificant dog! And look what it's doing to you!"

Maybe what I need is a change. Supposing I quit my job – or better still, just don't show up one morning. Supposing I vanish. Get into my car and drive somewhere. Yes – and mother? Who will look after her? But supposing (you can't help the thoughts that come into your head!) – supposing I... *abandon* my mother. Does this prove I'm evil? Or does the fact that I haven't yielded to these dreadful thoughts, haven't carried them out, prove I'm good? I don't know, I don't know! Lord, show me the path...

My boyfriend (for want of a better word) mocks my belief in God. He says the obvious things. "Look at the world – look around you! Pick up a newspaper! Would the sort of God you Christians believe in have created such an awful, unholy, wretched mess? And expect to be praised for it, yet?"

"Yes," I say, "but would you and I love each other if there were no God?"

That shuts him up – not because he loves me so deeply that such a love is inconceivable without a divine origin, but because he prefers to have me think that he does. Why, I wonder? It's not my money he's after – I have none, and he knows it. But it's true that he is somehow terrified at the thought of losing me, though he has two other girlfriends that I know about (he doesn't know that I know) and probably others that I don't. Is he terrified of losing them too? Probably. He's insecure to that degree. A strange man, my boyfriend. We've known each other since junior high school. I hated him. He used to sit behind me and pull my hair.

As usual, Mayumi sidles over to my desk at noon sharp and says, "How about a bite to eat?" Mayumi is someone else I knew in junior high school. It's pure coincidence that we work in the same office. We weren't really close as children, though we were in the same after-school volleyball club, and during the years I was away we naturally lost track of each other. When I came back and applied for the job there she was, an employee in good standing. Her recommendation had a lot to do with my being hired. There were many applicants. Our employer is the City of Otaru. Public sector jobs are in great demand. Every vacancy brings hordes of candidates hankering after a secure and easy life. Mayumi is four months pregnant and will soon be leaving. Just the other day the head of our department asked me if I would be willing to replace her. It would mean additional responsibilities, and additional pay. I promised him an answer by the end of the week.

"I'm in the mood for pizza," she says.

"How can you eat that greasy stuff with a baby, an embryo – "

"If my doctor has no objections, why should you? He said I can eat anything I want."

"I don't trust doctors."

"No, you put all your trust in God, I know."

"Listen," I say after the waitress has taken our orders, "this guy comes up to me on the street this morning and asks me if I'm Yuri Kawai."

"Again?"

"I must really look like her, since it keeps happening. Don't you think?"

"I don't see it. Honestly. Not at all."

"Me either. Anyway, something strange came over me, I'm not sure what exactly, and I said, 'Well, yes, as a matter of fact...'"

"No!"

"Crazy, eh? You should have seen him! He – my God, the power these celebrities have! It was all the poor fellow could do to stammer out a request for an autograph. So flustered he could hardly get a notebook out of his knapsack for me to sign."

"Student?"

"I guess. And then, turning red as a crab from the strain of gathering up his courage, he says, 'Can I... can I... this evening... buy you a drink?'"

"How'd you get rid of him?"

"I told him I'd meet him by the canal at six."

"No! Emi, you didn't!"

"I did!"

"Emi, don't go."

"Why?"

"I don't know. I have a bad feeling. Pregnant women, you know, are peculiarly sensitive. Please, Emi. Don't go."

"Mayu, if you'd *seen* him – "

"Pizza all dressed" – here's our waitress, setting down Mayu's pizza. Looking at it, I feel as if I'm the pregnant one, having an attack of nausea. "I'll bring you your salad right away," says the waitress, as though to reassure me.

At five I call my mother. "I'll be late," I say. "Overtime."

"Overtime!"

Mother's no pushover. Alzheimer's dulls the faculties of most people, but seems to have sharpened hers. Actually, no, she doesn't have Alzheimer's, she's just... well, not as young as she used to be. With age, I guess, your sense of perspective changes. What was important no longer seems so; instead, trivia becomes magnified out of all proportion. She used to read newspapers, magazines, books; she knew what was going on in the world; she wrote letters to the editors of the national newspapers – one of which, I remember, came up for discussion in my high school civics class. Now she reads nothing – having outgrown all that, I suppose – and is perfectly indifferent to the world outside our house; but what goes on *inside* the house, including my routine comings and goings, she knows with minute exactitude. She knows I don't work overtime, and immediately senses a false note in my rather hastily contrived excuse.

"Yes," I say, "the computers crashed this afternoon, they were down for two hours, we all have to work late."

"Tsk, tsk," grins Mayumi when I finally put down the phone. "Lying to your mother."

I close my eyes. "You know that girl in Kanagawa who murdered her mother? I know just how she must have felt."

"Saitama."

"Eh?"

"It was in Saitama, not Kanagawa."

"All right, Saitama. You don't know how lucky you are."

Mayumi's mother is dead. Her face clouds ever so slightly. It was a tactless remark, of course, and I am immediately sorry.

"I didn't think so when I was fifteen," she says.

"I'm sorry, Mayu, really." Lord, show me the path!

It's five fifteen and I'm to meet him at six. For the first time it occurs to me that I don't know his name. Nor, for that matter, can I remember his face – it was insignificant to that degree. This is stupid. Maybe Mayu's right. Maybe I won't go. Not because I'm afraid, but because what I crave – really crave – is not company but solitude. Is it possible, in this age of national government databases, biometric IDs, DNA testing, security cameras everywhere and whatnot, to vanish into some rabbit hole, or black hole, or Isle of Monte Cristo... in short, to give birth to yourself as an adult and start life all over again? Is it possible? Oh, to wake up one fine morning and find myself all alone in the world! No mother, no boyfriend, no job... And no name. Amnesia! Lord, strike me with amnesia!

The church I attend is two blocks from City Hall. It is a tiny stone building, very un-Japanese; if anything, it reminds me of Holland, or Denmark; not so much of anything I saw there as of something out of Hans Christian Andersen, or... what's the name of that Dutch story? Hans Brinker. In fact the minister, Father Kramer, is a South African, a massive man, tall and stout, as large as his church is small, with clear blue eyes and a vast blond beard that covers the knot of his tie. His size belies his gentleness, his soft-spoken

manner, his ready smile – a dazzling smile, really;
yes, there is power in a smile like that; I'm almost
tempted to say it's a gift from God. Do I sound
like I'm in love with him? Maybe I am. Maybe I
joined his church hoping he would seduce me.
Psychoanalysis, I believe, reduces everything we
do to motives of that sort – rightly, for all I know.
Anyway, he hasn't, though he lives alone, his wife
apparently having left him years ago; his interest
in me – for he does take an interest in me – is
purely that of shepherd to sheep; his guidance is
invaluable to me; I genuinely believe that without
his help I might, around the time I was fortunate
enough to meet him, have had a nervous
breakdown, or committed suicide, or murder; and
that with his help, one day, I will come to know
God.

We met at City Hall. He'd come to renew the
alien registration card every foreigner is obliged
to carry. That isn't my department, but I'm the
one he happened to approach, and I directed him
to the right wicket. We fell into a bit of talk. His
Japanese is perfect, or very nearly so. Later it
struck me that he probably knew quite well
where the alien registration section was, and
approached me on purpose because he sensed
some trouble in me. He has that kind of insight.
Without any unnatural emphasis, he told me
where his church was and invited me to drop by
if ever I felt like it. He smiled, bowed slightly, and
went about his business. I went to see him that
very day, after work. At first I felt a little self-
conscious about taking him up on his invitation

so immediately – what would he think? Would he be proud of his power? Or would the *psychoanalytical* explanation occur to him? But I soon laid my doubts to rest. They were, after all, so petty; there was too much at stake for that kind of nonsense.

———————

He comes out of his office to greet me as though I am the one person on earth he'd been sitting there wishing to see. He has that way with everyone, I know, but it never occurs to me on that account to question his sincerity.

"Father, is it permitted to pray for amnesia?"

"Amnesia!" He laughs. It is the laugh of a seaman – yes, a seaman; though why that of all metaphors should strike a woman who has never dealt with seamen or heard one laugh, I don't know.

"Hold your horses!" he says, still laughing. "Let's get to know each other first. Let me usher you into a chair, offer you some iced barley tea..." He is amused at the urgency with which I've sprung the unexpected question at him; his amusement is contagious; I can't help smiling myself as I follow him into his office.

"Amnesia!" he says again as he hands me my tea. "And why – "

I am mortified to suddenly find myself in tears – where could they have come from? "Father... father..."

"Emi-chan, what - ?"

He reaches behind him for the box of tissue paper on the desk, and hands it to me. I take one, raise my glasses, dab my eyes, blow my nose. What a spectacle I'm making of myself. "I'm sorry." I force a smile. "I don't know what came over me."

"Are you all right?"

"Yes. Yes, apart from being terribly embarrassed."

"Embarrassed? Here? My dear, in this office, in this church, there is no such thing as embarrassment. No such thing. Embarrassment withers in this atmosphere. It crumbles, it can't survive. There. It's gone."

"It's just... not like me to lose control of myself like that."

"It doesn't hurt, you know. Tears are therapeutic – 'tears such as angels weep,' as Milton said. He or she from whom God withholds the gift of tears... but what's this about amnesia?"

"Father, I want to forget everything! Forget who I am, where I come from, the people I know, the... I want to wake up one morning and start life over again!"

"Well, do so then."

"Pardon?"

"Do so."

"How?"

"My dear, it is within the power of all of us to be reborn."

"Through faith, you mean."

"Certainly through faith."

"I know, but... Father... do you know Yuri Kawai?"

"The singer? It'd be hard to live in Japan and not know her, don't you think?"

"Have you seen her?"

"Yes, on TV, in the newspaper. An 'idol,' they call her. 'Aidoru.' It's rude of me to say so, but sometimes I do wish the Japanese would leave the English language alone, unless they're prepared to learn it properly."

"Do I look like her?"

"Look like her! You! No. Emi-chan, surely you don't – "

"No, Father, no. You misunderstand me. I don't mean I *want* to look like her, it's just that... somehow I keep being *mistaken* for her. She's from here, you know, and I'm constantly being stopped on the street: 'Are you Yuri Kawai? Aren't you Yuri Kawai? You're not Yuri Kawai, are you?'"

"But why? That's incredible! I look at you now, and... no, there's not a trace of resemblance, not a trace!"

"This morning a boy asked me and... I don't know, I don't know what came over me... I said yes."

"Emi – "

"I'm to meet him at the canal at six." I glance at my watch. "It's ten past six now. Tell me what to do, Father. Be a father to me. I never knew my own father. Tell me what to do!"

All this time I've been seated on a kind of armchair, with him on his feet, hovering over me as if afraid I'll bolt, or dissolve into my component elements, or... I don't know what. But now abruptly he draws himself up to his full height and, seizing his hat from the coat rack, says, "Come. We'll meet him together."

———

Imagine my surprise when Father Kramer recognizes him before I do. "You!" he bursts out, laughing his rolling seaman's laugh. "You!" The boy just about jumps out of his skin. He'd been sitting, or rather perching, on a sort of guardrail lining the canal. The water gleams in the setting sun. Tiny fishing boats, moored to the quay, bob up and down, their sails rippling in the early evening breeze. It's suddenly chilly, and though I laughed at myself this morning for wearing a sweater, now I'm glad to have it.

Is this the boy? It's funny – the only thing about him that seems familiar is his knapsack, the little purple knapsack from which he withdrew the notebook he had me sign.

"Segawa, Segawa, I'm surprised at you!" the father is saying. "What is the meaning of this? Eh? Yuri Kawai! You ought to be ashamed of yourself!"

"But Father, what have I done?" Segawa, having got over his initial astonishment, is smiling; it is characteristic of the father's manner – perhaps I should call it his art – that he can rebuke someone in all seriousness, and be taken seriously, and yet provoke neither anger, nor resentment, nor embarrassment, but a smile. He spoke truly when he said embarrassment withers in his presence.

"What have you done? I'll tell you what you've done. You have, without the one excuse that might have sufficed to exonerate you, that of blindness, mistaken this estimable young lady for Yuri Kawai, a no-talent, dime-a-dozen 'aidoru'! You have further shown yourself tasteless enough to admire Yuri Kawai – otherwise why would you have asked a girl you thought was her for an autograph? Eh? Well? Have you anything to say in your defense?"

"I – "

"Your punishment is to be left alone to face the lady's wrath, and if it consumes you, it's nothing less than you deserve!" His stride as he leaves us is so long and rapid that in the time it takes to formulate the thought to call him back and demand an explanation for such extraordinary behavior, he is already beyond the range of our voices.

"So," says Segawa with a shy smile, "you're not Yuri Kawai."

The jazz café we're sitting in is a converted stone warehouse a block south of the canal. Western-style stone buildings – warehouses, shops, banks adorned (rather comically in the eyes of scoffers) with pseudo-classical-Greek columns – are our city's main attraction, many of them lately converted into restaurants, museums, boutiques and the like. Built during a local economic boom a century or so ago, in Otaru's heyday as a gritty but thriving port, they draw tourists from all over Japan, and from abroad too – because, say what you like about phoniness, this style of architecture is unique in this country, and uniqueness is always intriguing. The solidity of stone is as exotic to us – I remember explaining this to some people I met in Paris who found the oohing and aahing of Japanese tourists a little overdone – as exotic to us as traditional Japanese wood-and-paper flimsiness is to Western tourists here.

"Look over there," I say, leaning forward and lowering my voice so that it can be barely heard above the music. (I'm no connoisseur and I could be wrong, but it sounds to me like Thelonious Monk.) "See that handsome sexy young man with the gray wool hat pulled low over his forehead? That's my boyfriend."

"Oh? Who's the girl he's with?"

"That's his little secret. We won't pry. No, I am not Yuri Kawai. I'm sorry to disappoint you."

"Oh no! I – "

"Well, to have deceived you, then, if you won't admit being disappointed. I am not always above being deceitful, though I believe I am fundamentally honest. For example, I am five years older than my boyfriend thinks I am. And how old are you, if you don't mind my asking?"

"Me? Twenty."

"I'm twenty-seven, and there are times I feel fifty. Tell me: how do you come to know Father Kramer?"

"Oh, it's a long story..."

"A long story well told won't strain my patience."

"I don't mean long in that sense. I mean... hard to explain."

"You mean none of my business."

"No!"

"Your face is as red as the tulips in my mother's garden. My mother goes into raptures over her tulips. Last Saturday afternoon as she gazed at them glowing in the sunshine she suddenly burst out, 'Just look at those tulips! They're blooming like roses!' I laughed, thinking she was making a joke, but my laughter only made her angry. What school do you go to? Otaru University of Commerce?"

"Yes, but I..."

"You what? What's the matter with you? You're not a child. Speak! Express yourself! Think of me as an older sister who's so far above you in age and experience that you can blurt out anything that's on your mind, anything, without being embarrassed – it won't matter because I'm not part of your world anyway and after this cup of coffee we'll go our separate ways and never see each other again. You see what I mean? But in the short time we're together I want you to feel free to tell me everything, even the things you normally wouldn't dream of telling anyone else."

"I don't want to go into business."

"That's something you wouldn't dream of telling anyone else?"

"No, I mean... I was saying before... I go to Otaru University of Commerce, but..."

"Ah, I see. Well, what do you want to 'go into'?"

"I want to... I want to be a missionary."

"A missionary!"

"Is that so strange?"

"Well... it is an unusual ambition, in our day and age, yes."

"I know."

"I begin to see the connection to Father Kramer."

"Hey."

My boyfriend has joined us. We're at a small round wooden table for two, and he's squatting on his haunches, his chin resting on the edge of the table. Segawa shifts his chair slightly – the legs grate against the stone floor – in order to give him a little more room.

"Who's your friend?" he asks, ignoring Segawa and looking straight at me with an insolent smile that would look good on a fifteen-year-old but on him looks idiotic – not that it would occur to him to suspect as much; self-doubt is not within my boyfriend's emotional range. That's what I once liked about him.

"Who's yours?" I retort.

The piano piece tinkles to an end; now horns are sounding. African, I would judge from the rhythm.

"A client."

Is he being funny? Maybe not. He's a truck driver for Takkyubin, the parcel delivery firm. That's his day job, and entertaining 'clients' doesn't come into it. Does he have a night job too? Pimp? Gigolo? Host club host? He's handsome enough. Why shouldn't he make money off his body, if he can? We've never really discussed money, but now that I think of it, he always seems to have an unlimited supply of it. Strange that it never made me wonder before. What an erratic, capricious instrument the human mind is! And we talk of reason! Sometimes I imagine God idly dropping random thoughts into our heads, just to see how we'll react – and that's what we call thinking.

"Vanish," my boyfriend says, turning now to Segawa and looking at him through sleepy, half-closed eyes. Then, to me, "I delivered a package to her. She insisted on buying me a cup of coffee."

I would have expected Segawa to slink away – he seems the slinking-away type – but he makes no move to do so, and if there's any tension in him at the thought of what my vaguely thuggish-looking boyfriend might have in mind, he doesn't show it.

"Well," I say to my boyfriend, "suppose you go on with your evening, and let me go on with mine."

"No," he says, "your evenings belong to me." Turning again to Segawa, he says, "Coffee's on me, but time's up. On your way, young man."

"Not at all," says Segawa, his voice quiet, his calm absolutely unruffled. "I'll settle my own bill, in my own time. But thanks anyway."

"An attitude like that can get you hurt, you know."

"It hasn't so far."

"You're late," says my mother, before I have even got the key out of the lock.

"You didn't have to wait up for me."

"You know I can't sleep – "

"Well you'd better learn, mother! I am twenty-seven years old, old enough to – "

"You said you were working."

"Well?"

"It's thirteen minutes past two!"

"Yes, and I'm very tired. Goodnight, mother."

"Couldn't you have phoned? Couldn't you have – " Tears choke her. Her seamed, wrinkled, sagging face, ugly at the best of times, is positively hideous when she cries. Lately she cries often.

"I'm sorry. I would have phoned, but I thought you might be sleeping. Would you like me to make you some hot milk?"

"But what could have kept you until – "

"Mother, you've forgotten what it's like to be young. Otherwise you'd know that there are any number of things that could have kept me. There are many, many distractions out there in the world beyond this house. Go into the kitchen and wait for me. I'll be with you in a minute."

In my room upstairs, before I know it, I am on my knees, in tears, praying: "Lord, don't let me hate this woman, don't let me hate her, she's my mother, she hasn't had an easy life, You know that, and now she's old, old and sick... O Lord, melt the hatred I feel for her, it makes me afraid, afraid of what I could do. I picture myself flinging myself at her and strangling the life out of her, I picture it, I see it as vividly as I see anything in the so-called real world, and... don't let it happen, Lord, please don't let it happen. Strike me dead first, if You can't soften the hatred in my heart. But forgive me, that's blasphemy, of course You can soften it, You can do anything..."

I change into my nightgown, wash my face, brush my teeth, and go downstairs to find my mother has already heated up the milk and is pouring it into two cups – one for her, one for me. I don't want any, but she'll be hurt if I say so – she means it as a gesture of reconciliation. All right. A cup of hot milk won't kill me.

"I couldn't sleep, so I watched the eleven o'clock news. A bomb went off in a market in Baghdad. People running, screaming, screaming... In the middle of an alley was a leg, a leg, a child's leg..."

"You shouldn't watch the news. What for? It's not as if your seeing it will change anything."

"How could that God of yours permit it? How?"

"He's not 'that God of mine,' mother. He's God. His ways are beyond my understanding."

"I could never pray to a God who permits little children to be blown to pieces. I couldn't. I simply couldn't."

"Don't then."

"But you – "

"I cope with the things I don't understand in my way, you cope with them in yours. There's really nothing more to be said on the subject."

"Well, tell me about your evening then. Tell me about all those things I've forgotten, being no longer young."

"After work I went to see Father Kramer. He introduced me to one of his... his acolytes, I guess you'd call him... and we went out for coffee."

"You drank coffee until 2 a.m.?"

"No. We didn't drink coffee until 2 a.m."

"It's none of my business, of course..."

"Mother, supposing I tell you... that I witnessed a miracle tonight, an actual miracle. Would you believe me? Or will you think I've gone soft in the head?"

"None of the miracles I've heard about stand up to scrutiny."

"Father Kramer says life itself is a miracle. Our very existence is a miracle."

"If he's still saying that when he's my age, I'll be impressed."

"Mother..." I have a sudden idea. "Mother, will you let me introduce you to someone?"

"Who? Father Kramer?"

"No. Someone else. It's just possible meeting him will make a difference in your life."

———————

What made me blurt that out? Stupid, stupid! Now I'll have to follow through, invite Segawa over for dinner or something. Or maybe if I say nothing further mother will forget about it, or pretend she's forgotten. She's not crazy about company. Lately she keeps even her close friends at a distance – the friends she was once close to, I mean. My mother in her old age is turning inward. So it should be easy to wriggle out of this little corner I've painted myself into.

That's reassuring, but I still can't sleep. What time is it? Four seventeen, says the alarm clock at the head of my bed. And I have to be up at seven. Maybe I'll call in sick today. It won't be a lie. I *am* sick. My eyes are burning, my head is fogged. Am I feverish? I feel my forehead. Yes, maybe I do have a fever.

The next thing I am aware of is the buzzing of the alarm. Did I sleep? I must have, and yet I have no memory of drifting off, or of dreaming. The last thing I remember is touching my forehead to see if I have a fever. But the clock says seven, and morning sunlight streams in through the paper shoji screen. My sleep, such as it was, didn't refresh me exactly, and yet I don't feel tired either. "Oh, to disappear, to disappear, to disappear!" The words sound in my brain until the repetition renders them meaningless, mere noise. I slide open the shoji and look out into the garden, at my mother's tulips and the various other flowers she's planted. It's strange. People who love flowers are usually happy. Especially if they're as good at growing them as my mother is. I personally am indifferent to flowers. I don't even know the names of most of the ones my mother raises. Anyway, that general rule, if it is one, obviously doesn't apply to her. So why does she bother? Habit?

———

This canal of ours, now the core of the tourist area, is a prettified version of what a hundred years or so ago was a real port, a major one, the hub of Japan's grain trade with Europe and Russia. Back then, they say, the sea was so thick with herring you could practically scoop them out with your hands. Then spawning patterns changed and the fish disappeared. Commerce-wise, the ports at Yokohama and Kobe grew, and Otaru's shriveled. In the 1940s and '50s the canal was filthy, littered with the hulks of abandoned ships. I've seen pictures of it. During my childhood there was an epic struggle between those who wanted to fill it in and make a road, and those who wanted it preserved as a historical monument. My mother was an active campaigner among the preservationists. She attended rallies, made speeches. It went on for years. In the end there was a kind of compromise – part of it was filled in, part of it preserved and gentrified.

It's a nice place, even if a bit lacking in what might be called authenticity. I like to stroll along it early in the morning, before work, before the tourists invade, watching the fishing boats bob up and down and taunting myself with impossible dreams of maybe just helping myself to a boat and sailing away. Imagine: I grew up in a port city, a fishing city, and yet I've never ever been on a boat; I don't know how to sail, or how to fish, or even how to swim. The price one pays, I guess, for growing up without a father. Mine left when I was two. We never heard from him again.

I look at my watch: 9:30. If I'm going to work I should start heading that way now. If not, I'd better call. I reach into my handbag for my cell phone, but can't quite make up my mind to dial the number. Not that Nakano-san would make an issue of it. He's very understanding that way. He's not an old man, only in his forties, but his hair went prematurely white and he makes a great show of treating the younger staff as his grandchildren.

What will Mayumi think when she sees my empty desk? That my "Yuri Kawai" adventure got me into precisely the sort of trouble she foresaw; that my imprudence got me raped and murdered? She'll rush down to the canal at lunchtime, expecting to find my nude battered body floating in it. Or she'll ask Nakano-san if he's heard from me, and he'll tell her I called in sick, which will hardly reassure her.

Strange, these seagulls. They seem unusually excited – unusually numerous too - as they wheel overhead, squawking, screeching... What's on their minds? The crows too. So many of them! And other birds. I don't know much about birds – their names, habits, breeding patterns. It never really occurred to me before to be curious about them. They go their way, I go mine. But this morning I sense a kind of malevolence in their cries and their restless hovering. There's one kind of bird whose chirping sounds like, "Over there down the road! Over there down the road! Over there down the road!"

Segawa. Wasn't he magnificent last night? The way he faced my boyfriend – neither brave nor cowardly, neither defensive nor aggressive, just... calm, natural – until my boyfriend... what's the expression I'm looking for?... Until my boyfriend was *disarmed*. I was sure there'd be a fight, and I have seen what my boyfriend is capable of in that regard: once in a bar a guy was coming on to me in an unpleasantly persistent way, and my boyfriend just *wasted* him, as the Americans say. He's got fists like greased lightning. At one time he thought of being a pro lightweight boxer, and probably could have made his mark; he just didn't have the discipline, that was his trouble. Anyway, I shudder to think what he could have done to poor Segawa, if it had come to that – Segawa, by the look of him, has never been in a fight in his life; it would have been horrifying, ghastly, and yet he showed not the faintest sign of being afraid, or even of being aware that he was in danger. It was uncanny. What accounts for it? What quality does he possess that saw him through? Is this what's meant by Christian meekness?

The beep of a horn jolts me out of my reverie. It's my boyfriend, in his Takkyubin truck. He leans over, flings open the passenger door, pats the seat beside him. "Get in," he says.

I do. He sets the truck in motion even before I've closed the door. The radio's on. A woman whose voice is a high-pitched squeal is delivering a weather report. It is going to be hot-hot-hot! she says, as though relishing the prospect, not so much of heat but of being a witness to living meteorological history.

"Take the day off," says my boyfriend. "We'll drive to the beach and swim naked in the sea."

"I can't swim."

"You'll drown and I'll rescue you. I'm a qualified lifeguard, you know."

"You'll drive to the beach in *this*?"

"Would that embarrass you?"

"No, but it might get you fired."

"Let me worry about that. Call your office, tell 'em you're sick."

"I can't, I have – "

"Piles and piles and piles of work, I know, and the city would crumble into dust if you didn't dig in your heels and pull up your socks. Seriously, you don't look well."

"I didn't sleep."

"No? Not even after you got home?"

"My mother was up. I made her hot milk..."

"Let's get married, Emi. We'll make a baby who'll grow up and make us hot milk when we're

101

old and can't sleep. It's a pretty picture, don't you think?"

"Drive me to work, Yu. Really, I have to – "

"That Segawa character. I wonder if he knows how lucky he is. I mean, I wonder if he realizes how... how thin the line is between life and death. A man like him blunders into an encounter with a man like me, and... seriously, now. One blow, one blow is all it would take. That's how fragile the thread is that binds us to life."

"What's your point, Yu? What are you trying to say?"

"Nothing, just... I wonder if he realizes, that's all."

He drops me off at City Hall and drives off without a word. I climb the steps and stand at the door, unable somehow to bring myself to open it and step once and for all into the working part of the day. It is a grand and imposing building, more worthy of a national parliament than of a backwater municipal office. It should give those of us who work there grand ideas, but it doesn't; if anything it has the opposite effect. It shrivels us, makes us narrow, conventional. Before I'm aware of what I'm doing I've taken my cell phone out of my bag and am inputting the number. I recognize the voice of the woman who answers, an elderly woman "grown grim in the service of her city," as Mayumi likes to say. She has a good heart for all that. "Seki-san, it's Emi. I'm not feeling well, I have a fever, I've tried but I just can't drag myself out of bed. Would you mind telling Nakano-san?"

——— ——

From Otaru Station, there are only two places to go – east to Sapporo, or west to Yoichi. My momentary sense of freedom evaporates. At Sapporo of course you can take a train to anywhere in Hokkaido, but... I remember in Europe, the States, Canada, the sense you have of having a whole continent, the whole world, at your feet; you can walk into a station not having any particular destination in mind, board a train for you hardly know (or care) where, and wake up hours later in a totally strange, totally unknown place, having no business or no acquaintances there, maybe not even speaking the language... What made me come back to Japan? It's so narrow here, so cramped, so confined. It's like a straitjacket, this country. Why didn't I stay abroad? Was I so homesick? Yes, oddly enough I was. I missed my mother, my boyfriend. It's incomprehensible to me now, but true all the same. I went abroad for the first time when I was sixteen. It was my mother's idea. This is years ago, of course; both she and I were different people then. Worried that I was becoming too attached to her, she decided to foster my independence by enrolling me in a high school in Montreal. My mother went with me as far as Tokyo. I'll never forget our farewell scene at the departure lounge at Narita Airport. I cried and cried. "I don't want to go! Take me home!" My mother cried too, but there was no going back on arrangements that had been difficult enough to make. "Come, you're not a baby anymore!" sobbed my mother.

Despite that ominous beginning, my year in Montreal was wonderful. I found I had a flair for languages. I learned English, French, even a bit of Yiddish, my host family being Jewish. I made friends, partied, lost my virginity, sampled this drug and that. The school year ended, summer came, and instead of going back to Japan as I was supposed to, I spent a month hitch-hiking, at first with two friends, later all alone; I got as far as Vancouver and would have turned south, or north – what difference did it make? - but my mother's patience was at an end; she began to fear her experiment had been *too* successful, that I had become *too* independent; she refused to send me any more money and insisted I come home immediately.

I did, but couldn't settle down. I went to university, dropped out, got a job, quit, went back to school, became interested in ancient Greek drama, then in the ancient Greeks generally. I read Aeschylus, Sophocles, Plato. I quit school again, got another job, saved up some money – and went to Greece. I picked oranges, picked olives...

"Emi-chan!"

"Father Kramer! What – " I break off, sensing the stupidity of the question. He lives in Zenibako, halfway between Otaru and Sapporo; he takes the train to Otaru every morning. What *he's* doing here is obvious; the real question is, what am *I* doing here? He asks it, in a slightly different form: "You're not working today?"

"No, I – I took the day off."

"Where are you going?"

"Where? I don't know…"

"I'm on my way to visit some people who might interest you. Why not come along, if you've nothing better to do?"

"I… thank you, Father, but just now I think… I think I'd rather be alone, if that's all right."

"'Alone, alone, all, all alone,/ Alone on a wide wide sea!' Are you sure?"

"No! I'm not sure of anything!"

"Of course not. Only fools are. Come."

"Who said that, Father? Those lines you just quoted."

"Coleridge."

"Of course. The Ancient Mariner. I remember. I studied it in high school. I was thinking about high school just now…"

"These people I'm going to see. They're a family – an extended family – of Kurds from Turkey. They've applied for refugee status, but the Japanese government seems determined to deport them, despite a very strong likelihood they'll be arrested and tortured. The father is active in Kurdish nationalist circles. I bring what comfort I can, though obviously it's not much. Why is Japan so… so inhospitable? All developed countries take in refugees – why not Japan? True, they're here illegally in the sense that they've overstayed their visa. People on the run can't always stick to the letter of the law. Other than that, they're model citizens, hard-working, tax-paying... They all speak Japanese. The youngest child, a girl of six, was born here and speaks no other language. Come along, I'm sure they'll be pleased to meet you."

"No, Father, forgive me, but... you see, the reason I'm not at work today is that I called in sick, and I really am feverish. The fact is, I'm not even altogether sure how I came to be at the station. I was going home..."

"Good God!" Father Kramer touches my forehead. "You're burning! Let's get a taxi, I'll see you home..."

"Please, don't trouble. I'll take a taxi myself. People are waiting for you. How I wish I were like you, able to do some good in the world..."

"We can all do good in the world. But we'll talk about that another time. Go. Are you sure you can manage on your own?"

"Of course."

"Let me at least see you into a taxi."

"There's a whole fleet of them just outside the station. I'll be fine, really. Thank you, Father. Thank you for everything."

My mother is in the garden, scarcely visible under her vast straw sunhat, ministering to her flowers. She grows vegetables too – beans, potatoes, pumpkin, probably other things too;

I've forgotten. All summer long our salads come straight from her garden. She looks up in surprise as the taxi pulls up and I get out. "What are you doing here?" she says.

"I'm not feeling well, I have a fever, I'll go straight to bed and to sleep, if you don't mind."

"If you kept regular hours instead of – "

"Later, mother, later! You can lecture me later. For now, just… pretend I'm not here, ok?"

"Take two Bufferins, they'll bring the fever down."

"Yes, all right."

"And Emi…"

"What?"

"I'm sorry if I seem to you a fussy old woman…"

"Good night, mother."

"Do you need any help?"

"No."

———

There are no curtains in my room, only the shoji screen, which barely dims the daylight. Somewhat unsteadily, I get out of my clothes and into my pajamas, and crawl into my futon. I close my eyes, and everything seems to go not dark but red. I am in a burning desert, the sun beating down on me, my throat parched. Sand, sand everywhere. I've never been in a desert – why should this feverish vision of one be so real? Bufferin – yes, mother was right, I should have taken a pill, I should… no, I can't… I can't bear the thought of getting up. Suddenly I'm shivering. Before I was hot, now I'm cold. I pull the quilt up over my head. Now it is night in the desert, and strange beasts are baying. I hear them... howling, groaning... Why did God give the beasts voices and yet deprive them of intelligible speech? Nightmarish, nightmarish howling...

I wonder what Segawa is doing right now, right this minute. He's probably at school, dutifully attending a lecture he's not interested in. Is he thinking of me? I gave him my cell phone number; he said he'd call, but didn't say when. He attends business school to please his parents. It's not selfishness on their part; they want the best for their only son, and they think business is it. They have no idea – they don't even know that he's a Christian, let alone that he intends one day to go to Africa or India and dedicate his life to serving the poorest of the poor, "the wretched of the earth" – who said that, "the wretched of the earth?" It's from a poem, I think. "Alone, alone, all, all alone..." No, not that poem. One day Segawa will sit his parents down, he said, and tell them the truth, but he shrinks from it; it will be a dreadful shock to them. I reminded him of Jesus' words about forsaking one's parents to follow Him. I spoke lightly, but Segawa did not smile; he only nodded and looked thoughtful. Yes, he is preparing a great work. A great destiny is in preparation for Segawa. You can see it in his face, his eyes. Do I love him? Am I in love with him? Is it possible? Supposing he asks me to marry him – to marry him and follow him to India or Africa, to minister to the poor, the sick... My God! I've bummed around Europe a bit and think I know life! What a joke! I know nothing, nothing, nothing! Yes, I will follow him! Yes! Without an instant's hesitation, I will follow him! Why, why doesn't he call? He's sitting in some dreary lecture hall, listening to some dreary professor drone on about interest rates, investment maximization; doesn't he know, doesn't he feel what's going on in my soul at this very moment? How can he *not* know, he being the cause of it?

Howling, moaning, groaning beasts! The desert night is freezing, freezing, as cold as the day is hot! I am exhausted but must keep walking; if I stop to rest and fall asleep I'll freeze to death.

———————

"What are you doing? What are you doing?" Mother is frantic. I wake up but am not in bed, I am... Mother is tugging at me, pulling me. "Are you mad?"

"Where are we?"

A dog is whimpering; it lies at my feet; its brown coat is all bloody; its whimpering is pitiful. Mother slaps my face, slaps me again. "You bitch, you... you demon!" She bends over the dog. I am sobbing, sobbing... My mother has never, ever hit me before. "Go home and call the police. Hurry!"

"What... what shall I tell them?"

She rises upright and glares at me. "Tell them the truth! That you carried this boulder from our garden and bashed a helpless, defenseless dog with it!"

Yes, there's the rock, and it really is almost big enough to be called a boulder. Did I carry it?

"Go! Maybe it can still be saved. And what will we say to Kato-san when he comes home? Well? What will we say to him?"

"We'll say..." I master my sobbing, master my daze, and face my mother. "We'll say that the groaning of that wretched beast of his drove me insane! Every day, day after day, night after night, that awful, ghostly, unearthly moaning! We'll say that I gave it something to moan about!"

"You're inhuman! If you won't call the police, I will!"

"Go ahead."

"Get into the house, quickly! Standing around in the street in her pajamas and bare feet... with a fever, yet! Go!"

Nausea, dizziness... "Mother, I'm going to be sick."

Somehow she gets me back into the house and into my futon. "Did you take two Bufferins, like I told you?"

"No."

"All right, wait, I'll be right back."

I close my eyes. Years pass, decades. Then mother comes back. "Here." She hands me the pills and a glass of water, and helps me sit up. I swallow the pills, sip the water. She pushes me gently back on the pillow, and lays a cool washcloth on my forehead. "Thank you mother, that's... that's wonderful..."

Sonoko

I

"You're a strange girl!" muttered my mother, shaking her head.

"Yes, I know, mother. Well, I can't help it."

I've given up arguing with her. She's too old; so am I. Once, not long ago, I asked her if she knew The Lady Who Loved Insects. She didn't, of course. It's a semi-classical tale of the 12th century, little known except to antiquarians like me. The lady in question is also "strange" – in refusing to blacken her teeth, for instance, or pluck her eyebrows bald, as women did then as a matter of course. I showed my mother an illustration I happened to have of a typical woman of the day – blackened teeth, plucked eyebrows and all; a rather grotesque little figure – and demanded, "So? Who's strange?"

No fool, my mother was not at a loss for a reply. Is she ever? "Not falling in with the current fashion," she said, "is one thing. But not being interested in... well... boys... men..."

"It is true. I am not interested in boys or men."

"Are you a lesbian?"

"No."

"I wouldn't mind if you were, you know."

"Your minding or not minding has nothing to do with it."

"My dear girl, you are... thirty-four years old! You can't be a child forever!"

"I am *not* a child! I have a job, I'm self-supporting... In fact I support you, I believe! How dare you call me a child?"

"My dear, my dear, don't shout at me, I am not..." Her voice quivered; she was near tears, and I was immediately sorry. "How can you shout at me, knowing... knowing..."

"Mother, I'm sorry."

"Who have I lived for, if not for you?"

"I'm not shouting... mother, listen to me, please..." But she would not, and flounced out of the room, leaving me alone with my thoughts – my guilty thoughts, my *strange* thoughts. The water was boiling, and I poured my tea. Sipping scalding tea with my eyes closed – sometimes I think... no, often... that that is the greatest happiness we humans can know on earth.

———

For all this talk of strangeness, outwardly at least I lead the most ordinary of lives. I live with my mother, work in a bank... need I say more? And yet, hard though I try to blend inconspicuously into my environment, I am aware that I do not quite succeed. My effort shows, that's the trouble. My co-workers, though friendly, look at me a little askance, as much as to say, "You are so ordinary! And yet..."

I was nine when my father died. On his deathbed he said to me, "I am an alien from outer space; say nothing to your mother." Was he delirious? Or joking? These are questions I can ask myself now, but at the time, I took him quite literally, even matter-of-factly. Maybe as a result I developed differently. What he said seemed no more fantastic than the reality that surrounded me; no more fantastic than that he was dying, or that I was living, or that ocean waves washed the shore, or that rain fell and flowers grew.

"Why," Reiko blurted out to me at lunch one day, "are you always alone?"

Reiko's desk is opposite mine. We work in the foreign exchange section, since we both know English.

"Alone! What do you mean? Who's alone? I'm sitting in a restaurant with seven people!"

There was scattered laughter, my own louder than anyone's. Reiko frowned.

"Do you know, Reiko-chan," I said, cutting her off before she could pursue her thought, "I had a dream about you last night."

"About me?"

"Yes, a very vivid dream. You were blind, but didn't know it, and you were crossing a street, a very busy street, and I was standing on the curb screaming 'Reiko! Come back! You'll be killed!' But you just laughed and went on your way."

"I was blind and didn't know it?"

"Yes. Strange, isn't it?"

"I don't want to be in dreams like that!"

"No, of course not, who does?"

"Have you ever had a dream about me?" asked Little Hajime, quite seriously, though smiling. A nice boy, Hajime; a loans officer, said by everyone to have a brilliant future ahead of him. We called him Little Hajime as a joke; he's nearly two hundred centimeters tall and very self-conscious about towering over everyone the way he does. He's asked me out several times, always accepting my refusal without resentment, even with a kind of grace, as much as to say – but sincerely, without irony – "Of course I know I'm unworthy of you." "Ask me now," I found myself thinking; "ask me right this minute and I'll say yes." But the moment passed; he was still too young to possess the kind of intuition the occasion demanded.

"No," I said, "but I can tell your fortune if you like."

"Please do."

"You will quit the bank at thirty and go to work for an NGO, building schools in refugee camps in Africa."

Reiko laughed and was about to say something, but, seeing the look of confusion on Hajime's blushing face, broke off and, blushing a little herself, turned to Old Man Harada sitting next to her and somewhat abruptly demanded a cigarette.

II

Friday night. It's been a long day and a long week, but now, finally, I am on vacation, and the crowded train I am boarding seems not so much what it is as a marvelous conveyance about to whisk me to a whole new corner of the universe. There's no hope of getting a seat, of course; well, it doesn't matter; in very little more than an hour I'll be home, in a hot, hot bath... ah! And then, first thing tomorrow morning, I will be off – not to France, where everyone, including my mother, thinks I am going – what do I want to go to France for? – but to a quiet little hot spring hotel barely two hours from home, there to hole myself up for an entire week with my various editions of the Tale of Genji, my dictionaries, my commentaries, and, in perfect solitude, enclose myself in the world of my choice, that of 11th-century Japan.

This is my invariable vacation routine: I tell everyone I'm going to the sort of place they would naturally expect a modern, single, financially independent woman to go – Europe, Bali, California – and then, having, in a manner of speaking, shaken myself free of them and their expectations, I abandon myself to the whims and fantasies that constitute my inner life, which has so little to do with my outer life that really, it is only in the purely conventional sense that they are lived by the same person, namely my "self!" Is there a freedom more complete than that of being beyond the reach of other people's thoughts? I don't believe there is.

An odd stir makes me open my eyes. There is general consternation, in the midst of which a shrill voice rings out: "This car is for women only!"

"Sorry, sorry..."

So that's it. A man has blundered into the women-only car. It happens from time to time. I open my eyes and fairly gasp. It is impossible to be mistaken. His head seems to float disembodied above the scene, and his flaming face reflects an agony of embarrassment. "Hajime-san!"

His mortification redoubles on hearing his name called, but as soon as he recognizes me he breaks into a smile. "Sonoko-san!" Then, in a comic parody of consternation, he pleads, "Save me!"

As best as I can make out in the confusion, three women in particular, office workers like myself by the look of them, are determined to take a serious view of the matter, barring his escape and preparing to hustle him off the train and report him to the station authorities as a molester.

"He's all right, he's harmless, he's a friend of mine," I shout as I force my way through the throng that separates us. One of the three who has hold of him is an especially grim specimen, the sort of woman who has clawed her way to the top in a man's world by taking no nonsense from anyone; she looks at me now with positive hatred; but I can be pretty tough myself when the situation calls for it; I stare her down and somehow get Hajime out of their clutches. The next thing we know, the train is gone and we're standing on the platform together, gaping at each other in mute astonishment. It's Hajime who breaks the silence. "Did that really happen?" he asks, blinking in his bewilderment.

"I'm not sure," I smile. We have not seen each other in some time. Six months ago he quit the bank and went to work for the Bank of Japan. He was head-hunted, and from Mr. Harada – "Old Man Harada," as we call him – I'd heard that he was doing very well indeed. "Oh yes," said Mr. Harada, the loose flesh on his face quivering at the slightest shake of his head, "with a mind like his, with a mind like his, he'll leave us all behind. You wait and see."

———

"Do you know," Hajime says to me as we nurse our drinks in a little bar near the station, "I just noticed something about you – noticed it for the first time. I'm asking myself how I could possibly have missed it before."

"What?" I ask.

"You don't dye your hair."

I laugh. "Well?"

"It's remarkable. Look around you. Show me one woman with undyed hair."

"It's too dark to see."

"Nonsense. I can see quite well. Why do women do it? Dye their hair, I mean. Of course, I can understand this woman or that woman doing it as a matter of personal preference, but when *everyone, everyone* dyes her hair, to me that says something about the society we live in, and what it says is, that society is sick."

"Surely that's going too far."

"Do you remember you once predicted that I'd end up working for an NGO in Africa?"

"Yes. Obviously I'm not much of a fortune-teller."

"I don't know. It may happen yet. I've been thinking about it. Thinking seriously. This society of ours is so... so narrow, so constricted..."

"Even at the Bank of Japan?"

He laughs. "Yes, even there."

I finish my drink and say, "I'm afraid I have to go now. I'm on vacation, you see. I'm leaving first thing tomorrow morning."

"Oh really! Where are you going?"

"France."

"Ah, merveilleux, superbe! Bon voyage. Sonoko-san... will you marry me? I'm serious. Wait. Don't answer now. Think it over, while you're in France, and call me as soon as you get back. Here's my card. I've always loved you, you know, but it's only now that I've found the courage to tell you. Where did that courage come from, I wonder? Never mind, don't speak. Adieu – for now. Call me as soon as you get back. Yes or no, as you please, but call me!"

He's gone before I quite know it, and now it's my turn to feel bewildered, not altogether sure where I am. Did the scene so vivid in my memory really take place?

———

My mother is waiting up for me. This is unusual. But she is in an unusual state. She is distraught. "Mother, what is it?" She can't find the words to tell me, and instead thrusts a newspaper at me. The headline refers to a junior high school boy who stabbed his mother to death and then beheaded her. There's been a wave of grotesque crimes of that sort lately. It's appalling, of course, and no doubt reflects something deeply wrong in our society – maybe even the sickness Hajime spoke of – but here is my mother, sobbing, sobbing... "I... I... I know her!" she manages to gasp at last.

"Know who, mother? The victim?"

She nods vigorously, hysterically.

I hang up my coat in the hall closet and scan the story. The victim's name means nothing to me. Her age is given as 49. That's rather old for the mother of a junior high school boy – or maybe not, given how late people are marrying and having children nowadays. In any case, she is ten years younger than my mother. What can their connection be?

"Who is she, mother? What is she to you?"

"She... she..." There is no getting anything out of her.

"All right, mother, take a pill, get some sleep, we'll talk about it in the morning."

——— ———

Mother understands, of course, that you can't just cancel a trip to France on the spur of the moment. "Go, go," she says to me over breakfast, after I wondered aloud whether she's fit to be left alone. "I'll be fine."

"But who is this woman, mother?"

"Nobody. I was mistaken. I used to know somebody with the same name, but she was my age, we played together as children, she moved to Osaka in fifth grade. You'd better hurry. You don't want to miss your plane."

"Are you sure you're all right?"

"Of course I'm all right."

——— ———

The hotel is nearly empty; I have it practically to myself – which of course is why I take my vacation in November. Japan is a crowded country. Privacy comes neither easily nor naturally. If you want privacy, you must seize the off-seasons. I remembered Reiko saying, with that faint grimace so characteristic of her, "Only Sonoko would think of going to France in November." But never mind Reiko. It's three a.m. and I am wide awake. I lie in my futon in the pitch-dark silence, in an unfamiliar room whose contours I do not know, staring up at a ceiling I can't see, thinking to myself, This is bliss. This is happiness. If only time would freeze now, this instant, and I could just lie here for all eternity, with no other thought in my head than this: Everyone on earth who knows me, everyone, without exception, thinks I'm in France, a country I've never been to, know nothing about, have no particular interest in, never seriously thought of going to... If that isn't as close as you can get, this side of the grave, to disappearing into another dimension, what is?

———————

"Well, Sono-chan! Let's talk. Let's get to know each other. How are you getting on?"

My father. He often comes to me in dreams. "You can't conceive what it is like here. The body, you see, is a prison. Once free of it, the soul expands to its natural dimensions, which are limitless, limitless. Words fail me. We don't use words here. We've no need of them. My one regret is that I was unable to take you with me. Even now I miss you. Do you know, sweetheart, that you are the only one I ever loved during my brief time on earth? It's true. I used to think I loved your mother, but after you came along... after you came along... I knew what *real* love is."

"Shall I die, then?"

"Don't say it like that. Say rather, 'Shall I liberate my shriveled, withered, half-starved soul?' And the answer, of course, is yes, if you have the courage."

"I have the courage."

"Are you sure? It is no easy passage we're talking about."

"You must help me, then."

"I will, child. I will."

"What must I do?"

"Reiko will murder you. You know, of course, how she loathes you, how jealous she is of you on Hajime's account."

"How will she murder me?"

"How does one woman murder another? She stabs her. She has already purchased the knife."

"Oh, father, really! Reiko? She's a fool, a weakling..."

"A weakling provoked is surprisingly strong, my dear – the more so if she is a fool."

"Do I provoke her? I don't mean to."

"Don't you? I'm not so sure about that. Sometimes I watch you, and... I'm not so sure."

———

I walk in the door to find my mother waiting for me – with a newspaper in her hand. "Raped," she says through clenched teeth and trembling lips. "On a train. On a *train*. And *nobody* so much as lifts a *finger* to help her."

"Mother, what kind of greeting – "

"And you," she shrills. "You go off, all by yourself, heaven only knows where, no way to get in touch with you... Don't you know what kind of world this is?"

"Mother, please, I've had a long flight."

"Don't you know – "

"I know, I know! Well, if you want to die just say the word, I'll strangle you and then kill myself. Failing that, this is the only world we have, so let's make the best of it and not work ourselves into hysterics over other people's misfortunes."

"But... but that poor girl... she could have been *you*! That could have been *you* it happened to!"

"It's not likely, mother. You needn't worry about me. I can take care of myself."

———

On my third day back at work, in the morning, I receive a phone call from Hajime. "You didn't phone me," he says. "I guess that's your answer. Still, I thought I'd... Won't you at least meet me for lunch?"

Reiko, sitting opposite me, looks up from her computer screen. It's obvious from the look on her face that she knows, or thinks she knows, who I'm talking to. Our eyes meet; she lowers hers. My heart sinks. Not that I'm afraid of her, but at the sight of her I feel such disgust, such a longing for solitude, such an aching, desperate longing...

For a week, for a whole, voluptuous week, it was mine, that solitude, and now, thrust back into the daily routine, I have yet to erect my defenses against its banal assaults. The Genji chapter I immersed myself in at the hot spring was "Akashi," my favorite in the whole tale. Genji, in exile at Suma, is visited by an aged, eccentric

123

monk come in a mysterious boat. Signs and portents suggest that the monk's daughter, whose life until then had encompassed sorrow upon sorrow, is destined for Genji and Genji alone. Genji accompanies the monk to the monk's home in Akashi. He finds the girl uncommonly reticent, but at last coaxes this whispered verse from her: *"You speak to one for whom the night has no end. How can she tell the dreaming from the waking?"*

Yes, her destiny was unfolding. In the course of time she would be the mother of an empress...

"Sonoko-san? Are you there?"

"Hajime-san." I speak the name loudly enough for Reiko to hear, and watch her flinch. "I'm sorry. I was daydreaming."

"How was France?"

"Very... very French."

He laughs. "Meet me for lunch, Sonoko-san. I must speak to you."

"Lunch?" Again I raise my voice for Reiko's benefit. Her eyes glitter; her face is pale. "With pleasure. Where?"

He names a restaurant I don't know, and tells me how to get there.

"One o'clock," I say. "Good. I'll see you then."

I hang up and, flashing Reiko a friendly smile, rise from my desk to deliver some papers to Old Man Harada.

The Concussion

Mavrin comes in to light the lamp. "Your trial's tomorrow," he says.

"My trial! Am I to stand trial?"

"That's what I'm told."

"But... but... it's mad! Since when does the victim stand trial? You know yourself..."

"I know nothing. Absolutely nothing."

Well, I'll tell you then. I was sitting at home when five thugs burst in, seized me, drugged me – "

"Please. Please."

"And the next thing I know – "

"Be reasonable. Who are you telling this to? I am a servant, an odd-jobs man. I light the lamps, sweep the floors..."

"How long have I been here?"

"I don't know. One loses all sense of time in this – "

"How long have *you* been here?"

Without answering, he turns his attention to the lamp. It hisses, sputters, smokes; then suddenly flares into a steady, if pale, glow.

"Tell me this at least. What am I charged with? What's the charge against me?"

Mavrin shrugs. "Evil thoughts, maybe."

———

The heavy door slams shut and I wake up. This is past a joke. What time is it? Two forty-two? I grope for the clock at the head of my bed, press down on the top to light it up... Two forty-four. Every night: same dream, same time. What does it mean? Should I see a psychiatrist? Should I call Ron? I've been putting it off and putting it off, but today, I think, I will call him. I can't go on this way, I can't...

———————

Suddenly it's morning, a bright, sunny morning; even the drawn curtains can't keep out the sunlight, so eager is it to wish me good morning and usher me into this brand new day! Who was it – some poet or philosopher – who said, "A new day, a new life," or words to that effect? A new day, a new life! And what of last night's dream: Mavrin, the dungeon? Mavrin – what an odd name. Where would that have come from, I wonder?

"Evil thoughts," he says. Evil thoughts. Impossible to tell, so expressionless is his face, whether he's being serious or ironic, whether he's laughing at me or, out of the goodness of his heart, offering me a hint as to where I should direct my research. Evil thoughts. Is *that* the root of what ails me?

There was that incident the other day on the train: the little girl who quailed at the sight of me. She let out a cry, buried her face in her mother's pale blue down jacket. I looked quizzically at the mother, who, blushing, explained: "Two years ago a foreign man exposed himself to her, she hasn't quite got over it. I'm sorry..."

"May I speak to her?" I asked.

"Yes, please."

"What is her name?"

"Maya."

"Maya-chan," I began... but got no further – what could I say? I simply could not think of a single thing to say! The hideous blankness of the mind as it churns in vain to produce the right word, the right phrase... The train was approaching a station, slowing to a stop. With a sheepish grin at the mother, who smiled as if to show she understood my predicament, I made a beeline for the door and got off. Where was I? I hardly knew. I don't know the city well, though I've lived in it most of my adult life.

Ron's name is not really Ron, it's Yasu – Yasuo. Why do I call him Ron? Well, back in the 1980s the Prime Minister of Japan was Yasuhiro Nakasone and the President of the United States was Ronald Reagan; they were on a first-name basis, calling each other "Ron" and "Yasu" – it became known as a "Ron-Yasu relationship," symbol of close ties between the two countries. What does that have to do with Yasuo Fukuda, my former probation officer? Nothing, nothing at all. He was a child in the 1980s; even when I knew him he looked more child than man. Anyway, his name, Yasu, just naturally suggested "Ron," and that's how I think of him; it's stupid, but I can't help it.

He's not a psychiatrist, though I think of him as one. He was a kind of psychiatrist to me. In another culture he might have been a shaman or a faith healer. It's not so much the advice he gives as his way of listening. I can't explain it. It's a natural gift he has, a gift for listening – at the root of which, maybe, is a gift for caring. He, for example, would have found something to say to little Maya. Or – more correctly – she would not have quailed from him in the first place. Even if he had been foreign. Even if he had been the twin brother of the man who... did that thing to her.

He, if anyone, would understand my dream. He would understand, and tell me what to do. Or rather, he would understand and say nothing, but his silence would speak volumes; it would comfort me and instruct me. Yes, if anyone can help me, it is Ron.

Still, I hesitate to call him. It's been ten years, or almost. Ten years. It's awkward to contact someone after such a long time. He probably thinks I'm dead – if he thinks of me at all, which he probably doesn't. Why should he? Yes, God has blessed me with a long life; I am six weeks shy of my eighty-seventh birthday. Of course, in our time many, many people live to that age and beyond – far beyond. Just the other day I read in the newspaper about the number of centenarians there are in this country. Twenty-something thousand I think it was. Still... after ten years, wouldn't my voice on the phone seem to him as a voice beyond the grave?

———————

"A new day, a new life" – I don't know who said it, but does it matter, if there's wisdom in it? And there is; I feel it. I look out my bedroom window on the freshly fallen snow sparkling in the sunshine, and I think to myself, "I've been born again." My years do not weigh heavily on me. I've never been sick in my life, I'm as strong as I ever was – a lot stronger, I think, than the flabby, slack-bellied salarymen I see on the train, men half my age who nevertheless look a lot closer to the grave than I feel myself to be. Suppose... hm! suppose to celebrate my rebirth I go skiing?

There's a forest-park (that's what they call it) right in the heart of the city, three train stops from the station nearest my house; I could be there in twenty minutes. It's a vast, vast expanse, with miles of trails, but I go off the trails, deep into the woods on the virgin snow; there's not a soul in sight, not a sound to be heard, except for the occasional bird or the sigh of the wind in the bare treetops... And poking through the snow are the coarse green leaves of the dwarf bamboo, trembling in the breeze as though they were dancing... It's hard to describe... I am not a poetic man, and yet there are times, as I tramp along on my skis, when I feel tears welling up in my eyes, yes, tears, and I think to myself: "This is it, this is pure beauty, and I, a plain man, nobody really, have been granted the privilege of beholding it." It is enough to make even someone like me, with no religion and no beliefs of any kind, almost want to bow down and worship.

Yes, to hell with Ron, to hell with Mavrin, to hell with all of them. I'm off to the forest.

———

Where am I? Not in the forest, that's plain. I am lying on a bed – a cot, rather – among milling crowds, noise – shouts back and forth mingled with what sound like recorded announcements. There are other cots too, with people lying on them, but there's no order, it's not a room; more like a corridor, the walls a pale, sickly green...

As a child I used to dream of being buried alive. I had forgotten; suddenly the memory comes back to me. I would wake up screaming, in terror; my mother would come to me... She didn't know what the matter was, and I was so young, I didn't have the vocabulary to explain... "Nurse!" – for I have oriented myself by now; no grave, this, but a hospital, and the woman sailing past me in her white uniform is unmistakably a nurse. "Nurse! What on earth am I doing here? How did I..."

"Sh! Lie down, calm yourself! I'll call the doctor."

She is gone before I can muster a reply.

A peculiar lassitude comes over me. Have I been sedated? It is strange: I see and hear as before, and yet... *not* as before, because the sights no longer bewilder me, the sounds no longer irritate; if it's possible to be *in* a place and yet *not* in a place at the same time, then I am here without being here, and if it's *not* possible, then... I simply don't know what!

———

Time passes and the doctor doesn't come; I've been forgotten, but, oddly enough (for I know myself to be not the most patient of mortals!) I don't mind; on the contrary, I am comfortable, content. I don't know that I have ever been more so, though my surroundings are anything but conducive to contentment – there is even, I notice now for the first time, someone somewhere moaning in what sounds like terrible pain, whether physical or mental I can't say. I hear this and recognize it for what it is, and yet – well, let her moan!

Supposing, the thought occurs, I've died, and this is eternity. Just lying here, wrapped in this... whatever it is I'm wrapped in... Looking on at this endless commotion which has nothing to do with me, hearing all this frantic clamor which, though all my life I've been peculiarly sensitive to noise, disturbs me not at all... Supposing the angel in charge (to borrow a Christian metaphor) were to approach me now and say, "I'm offering you a choice: you can remain here for all eternity, or you can go back to earth for ten more years of life. Choose!" Well, I'd hesitate, I admit, being somewhat attached to life, but in the end... yes, I think I'd choose to remain. I think –

"Mr. Nakajima?"

"Yes."

"How do you feel?"

The label pinned to his white uniform above the breast pocket reads "Watanabe." His hair is covered by a close-fitting cap, his mouth and nose by a mask, so that all I see of him, really, are his spectacles.

"I feel fine. Why am I here?"

"What is the last thing you remember?"

"The last thing..." What *is* the last thing I remember? Skiing – I was going skiing. To the forest. I remember going to the storage closet where the skis are, dragging them out... I remember putting on my jacket, the sound the zipper made (rather like a fart) as I zipped it up...

"Do you remember leaving your house?"

"Yes, and... I remember being on the street, and suddenly not being sure whether I had locked the door or not. I went back to check. I often do that; it's a sort of quirk of mine I guess you might say."

"And?"

"And..." I look at him in some bewilderment. His eyes behind the spectacles – perhaps it's the effect of the rest of his face being invisible – are intense and concentrated but otherwise devoid of expression; I can read nothing in them – except, perhaps, youth. He is a young man – or maybe not so young; at my age the word "youth" takes on an almost absurdly expanded meaning.

"That's all. The next thing I know I'm lying on a cot in bedlam, wondering how on earth I got here."

"I see."

"Would you be so kind as to tell me *what* you see?"

"My information is that a passerby found you unconscious on the street and called an ambulance. He assumed you'd had a heart attack, but the medics found nothing wrong with your heart. The best guess is that you slipped on a patch of ice and, in falling, struck your head. Are you in pain of any kind? Does your head hurt?"

"No... well... now that you mention it, yes, I do feel a... a kind of throbbing..."

"Yes, you'd better remain here overnight. You may have suffered a concussion, and it would be best..."

"Remain overnight? Here?"

My sudden panic is of course inconsistent with the peace and lassitude I was feeling a moment ago, but, inconsistent or not, the lassitude is gone and the panic very real. "No, that's impossible, I must... I have to..." I raise myself up on one elbow, and suddenly the dull throbbing becomes a searing stab of pain that sends me reeling back onto the pillow. I can imagine my expression as I gaze up at Dr. Watanabe. It would be one of offended surprise, as though to say, "Why have you done such a thing to me?"

"I'll have the nurse give you something to help you sleep."

———————

I sleep and yet do not sleep – it's difficult to explain. I am here and yet not here; me and yet not me. Still on the cot, I feel myself being wheeled somewhere – to the dungeon, perhaps, where Mavrin will be lighting the lamp. That's fine. Let it be there, or let it be somewhere else. For the first time it occurs to me to wonder about my skis. Did I have them with me when I collapsed? I must have – in which case, are they still lying there on the road? Or did someone take charge of them, or steal them? In I go, through a doorway or passage of some sort, and the cot comes to a halt. There is not a sound, not a movement. It is not dark, but it is not light either. It is as if – this is fantastic – as if light has assumed the role of darkness, that of concealing everything. I do not understand, but I tell myself, "I have had a concussion, I've been given a sedative; it is only natural that my perception of reality is skewed."

———————

"How do you feel?" asks Dr. Watanabe.

"Fine, perfect. Thank you for everything. With your permission, I will take my leave."

"Yes, certainly. But... tell me: do you live alone?"

"Yes."

"You've no family?"

"No."

"I confess that I would be easier in my mind about you if you did *not* live alone."

"Oh, you needn't worry about that. I'm used to living alone. I'm what's known as a natural solitary. I've lived alone all my adult life – since I was eighteen."

"Is that so? Well, being eighteen is one thing, being eighty-six is another. And you *have* had a concussion. That remains a fact to reckon with, though our tests show nothing amiss. Tell me: how is it you have a Japanese name?"

"I changed my name when I acquired Japanese citizenship."

"And how – "

"It's a long story."

"I see. I don't mean to pry, it's just..."

"Just what?"

Watanabe's eyes narrow; they take on a peculiar cast. He has realized something, made a connection. His face behind the mask must be registering intense surprise. "Nakajima... Shoichiro?"

I smile. "The same, at your service."

———

If you are wondering how it is I speak such pure, idiomatic Japanese, without so much as a trace of a foreign accent, the answer is simple: I was born here. My parents had come as missionaries. They ran a small neighborhood church – a cozy, intimate haven of cleanliness, friendliness and godliness. It was a great success. People dropped in as they would on a friend, and the entertainment, so to speak, consisted of prayers and sermons. The god of my parents' church was a nice guy, a helpful neighbor, a charming host; he wore his omnipotence lightly. He consoled those in need of consolation, encouraged those whose courage was flagging, congratulated those whom fortune had favored in some enterprise or other – gently reminding them, however, to take care because pride goeth before a fall and the mighty can be brought low as abruptly as they were raised high. This ironic tone I'm displaying is habitual with me when I recall my parents' church; it predates the awakening of my critical faculties; I must have been born with it.

Possibly I was also born with the passion for destruction that is now to become the theme of this story. Possibly irony and destruction go hand in hand. The following memory is vague but insistent; something like it must have happened. I would have been four or five at the time. An electric train set I'd been clamoring for materialized under the Christmas tree, and in due course ownership was conferred upon me. It would be misleading to say that my joy was mingled with, or tainted by, a secret wish to destroy it. No – rather, my joy *was* the secret wish to destroy it. It was Ron – Ron-Yasu – who, many years later, helped me understand that – not by explaining it but by listening to me with a certain expression on his face, an expression of which he was almost certainly unconscious.

Destruction... yes, in the course of my long life I have destroyed many things, the inexpressible joy that accompanied my rampages being intense enough, deep enough, to be called sacred. I am not joking, and you who laugh know neither joy nor sacredness; you don't even know that you don't know, because you think you *do* know. Your blind ignorance keeps you out of trouble, no doubt, but your lives are hollow. Never mind. I'm not here to argue with you, or to mock you, though, truth to tell, I do find you funny.

———

Here's something else Ron-Yasu's silence helped me understand, or at least suspect: that my destructiveness was rooted in a rebellion against my parents' god. My poor parents! Who wouldn't rebel against such a god? To bind yourself to a god like that is to doom yourself to the condition that sums up my parents' fate, and presumably that of their parishioners as well – innocence, which is to say, living death. For what is life if not a struggle against ever-encroaching Death, among whose other names are Obedience, Goodness, Love. Life! *Life* is what the human condition demands – unfettered life! God loves those who *live*. From those who merely obey him, or who merely love him, he turns his face in disgust. "Grow up!" he reproves them. "Do you think I created you to be children forever?"

137

And yet – I too was in love once... Even now, a certain tenderness steals over me as I recall that long-ago episode. I was eleven, and she... well, laugh if you like; she was my sixth-grade teacher. Miss Small. The name suited her to a T, because she was... well, I prefer the word petite, though the epithet more generally current among my classmates was dwarfish. Was she pretty? The only honest answer is no, she was not. Wherein, then, lay her beauty? In her helplessness. She was very young, I believe it was her first year as a teacher; certainly it was her first year in Japan; she was a black woman, from Jamaica; she knew no Japanese at all, and the Japanese kids, who made up half the class, were simply beyond her control. Among other childish tricks, they abused her obscenely in Japanese; she faced a class full of children shrieking with laughter at she simply knew not what.

A brief autobiographical note will clear up any confusion that may have arisen. My schooling until then had been in Japanese. I grew up speaking mostly Japanese; we spoke English at home, of course, but I spoke it, though correctly, almost like a foreigner, and it was to rectify that that my parents decided to place me in an international school. I don't remember how I felt about it at the time – probably I was indifferent. School was never to me what it was to other children, a venue of struggle, triumph, despair. Perhaps I never was a child in the ordinary sense. As the only foreign kid in a large Japanese school, I learned very early on to face down bullies.

Having once made such an example of a would-be tormentor that the others conceded my right to be left alone, I became peaceable enough – I was never one to look for a fight. As for my studies, I suppose I had a kind of knack for that sort of thing – book-learning and such – because, without straining my faculties I was perpetually at the top of my class. Great things were expected of me. Once the principal lamented to my parents what a shame it was that the Japanese system made it impossible for gifted children to skip grades. Maybe a sense that the system was holding me back had something to do with the switch to the international school. I really don't remember.

Japanese school, international school – it was all the same to me. As it happened, it was inscribed in the Book of Life that the international school was to be the backdrop to my fleeting role as poor Miss Small's knight in shining armor – that is to say, her lover, for I was no less.

It happened in this fashion: A boy named Yuji Otake, whom I can see in my mind's eye as clearly as though he were standing before me – his surname means "big bamboo," and it was as appropriate to him as Miss Small was to Miss Small – a doltish lout, as big at age eleven as a full-grown man, and almost as hairy; yes, I believe he had actually started shaving – this Otake abruptly and with no provocation interrupted Miss Small's timid explanation of the Pythagorean theorem to call out, in a voice that had already begun to change, "Shut your face, you black cunt!"

I seem to hear as I recall the scene a faint feminine scream – it would not have been Miss Small's because she would not have understood; one of the Japanese girls, then. But Otake's disciples – every boy like Otake has a band of disciples – quickly rallied, drowning whatever outrage and distaste there may have been in loud, vulgar, braying laughter. Fists pounded rhythmically on desks and a chant was struck up: "Black cunt! Black cunt! Black cunt!" I stole a glance at Miss Small's face, and the image that came immediately to mind was of a human being being roasted on a spit. It was the most intense, the deepest feeling I have ever had in my life; nothing, nothing in the seventy-five years that followed has come close to it. Maybe it was so deep, so intense, that it so to speak overloaded my emotional circuitry, and I have been numb ever since. A person can kill in an emotional state like that. All things considered, I am fortunate to have got through my life thus far without committing murder.

I sprang to my feet, strode over to Otake's desk and, before he was fully aware of my presence, I think, I slapped him hard across the face. I should mention that I was a runty little fellow, destined (as I think I obscurely realized) to grow into a runty little man. I was short and thin; at eleven I probably could have passed for eight; my external appearance gave no hint at all of my strength, and since coming to the international school I had been quiet and, so to speak, undestructive, so this sudden explosion on the part of so unassuming and mousy a kid would have come as a total shock to someone like Otake, whose only notice of me up to that time had been an occasional glance, hard to describe, which seemed to say, "You're prey and I'm hungry; just wait, your turn will come."

I slapped him again, so hard he cried out. He lunged for me but I was too quick for him. Darting behind his chair I threw a headlock on him which, as I tightened it, seemed to immobilize the rest of the class as much as it did him. "Now," I said – and I can only imagine how strange the grown-up words must have sounded in my piping childish voice, "I want you to go up to Miss Small, bow very low, tell her in English what you said, and apologize. Do you understand?" I tightened the headlock, and tightened it again, until I detected a feeble gesture which seemed to indicate compliance. I loosened my hold but did not release it. "Do you understand?" I said again, very quietly. "Yes," he gurgled.

———

Mavrin comes in. I gape at him. It is not lamplighting time; what is he doing here? "I've come for you," he says, his tone neutral as always.

"You've come for me? What..." I struggle to control my trembling voice. "What do you mean, you've come for me?"

"Your trial is about to begin."
"So there is actually to be a trial!"
"Oh yes, most definitely. Did you doubt it?"

———————

"Hello... hello? This is... is this the probation office? This is Nakajima, Nakajima Shoichiro, is Mr. ... Mr. Fukuda... Hello? Mr. Fukuda, Yasuo, he was my... Hello?"

He no longer works there, the young woman informs me. Two years ago, or was it three, he was transferred to Kagoshima, in the south of Kyushu. Kagoshima! Why there, of all places? He is Hokkaido born, Hokkaido bred, a passionate skier; why, he can't live in a hot climate! For a brief instant it seems as if all the injustice in the world has been condensed into this one trivial administrative decision which transferred the winter-loving Ron-Yasu to a place where there is no winter. He'll wither there. "Shall I give you the phone number of the Kagoshima office?" the young woman inquires. "Please, please," I murmur, and she reads it out, but I do not write it down. I can't escape the feeling, as I hang up the phone, that something major, something decisive has just happened, something that has irrevocably altered my destiny – I feel this, feel it intensely, though at the same time I know perfectly well that nothing at all has happened, that I can contact him as easily in Kagoshima as I can here, that he'll adapt easily enough to the new climate, and so on, and that if he doesn't it's his problem, not mine.

For the first time in my life a thought occurs to me: that it is time to end my life. It is strange, perhaps, that for all my ups and downs I have never, ever, not once, thought of suicide. Do I love life to that degree? Well, yes. Is that strange? Yes, I plead guilty to loving life – not to fearing death, mind you... although... Actually I was lying when I said I have never thought of suicide. I did think of it once... when? When I was eleven, and Miss Small moved back to Jamaica.

She vanished that very day. After lunch our class was temporarily merged with Mr. Richardson's. Mr. Richardson spoke no more Japanese than Miss Small, but he was a huge block of a man, a former American football player, though not a major-leaguer; the boys were terrified of him, though he never raised his voice – he never had to. A week later it was announced that Miss Small had, as I said, gone back to Jamaica and a new teacher would be coming. The new teacher duly came, and our education proceeded. Of the new teacher nothing need be said. She was a teacher, period.

It was a very bad time for me – although, preoccupied as I was with Miss Small, I never lost my position as the undisputed top student in my grade, and I doubt anyone – not my parents, not my new teacher, not my classmates – had even the faintest suspicion that I was passing through an emotional crisis. I was that way – when not actively making my presence felt I became, in a manner of speaking, invisible. Years later I came to know of a Japanese sage of the 13th century, Enroku by name, of whom it was said that he had attained a level of quietness so profound that he actually became invisible. I'm no sage, but I did have the capacity – and still do – to sit quietly for hours on end, not stirring, scarcely breathing. Once, I remember, I came out of my room and met my mother in the hall. "Oh!" she gasped. "I'd forgotten all about you!" Yes, that is what I wanted. I wanted, without ceasing to exist, to have my existence forgotten.

I had a world atlas in my room, and found Jamaica in it, and spent hours staring at it: a tiny egg-shaped island, set in a vast blue sea. Where in Jamaica would she be? Kingston? Montego Bay? "One day when I'm old enough," I told myself, "I'll go there and find her and... and marry her." What made me think of suicide was the suspicion – no, the certainty – that I never *would* be old enough – the gulf between me and adulthood seemed so hopelessly, hopelessly vast. Why had I been born a child? It was like a deformity I had to learn to live with.

———

Why am I scribbling these rambling, incoherent scraps? I'm not sure. The immediate impetus was the recurring dream about Mavrin and his damned lamp – and then, it just acquired a momentum of its own. If nothing else, it's an occupation; it keeps me busy, it's something to do.

I am 87 years old. Maybe I should write my autobiography? I am joking, of course.

———————

My thinking about suicide matured to the point of settling on a building from whose roof, twelve stories up, I would jump to the thoroughfare far below. In a kind of ecstasy I pictured myself hitting the pavement and being driven over by vehicle after vehicle until nothing was left of me but a bleeding shapeless pulp, lifeless and yet not – for of course it is impossible to picture ourselves truly lifeless. Why did I settle on that particular building? It was fated. The bus stop where I changed buses to go to school was right in front of it. It was a conspicuously tall building, the tallest one around. And its name, to my childish sense of irony, was irresistible: The Japan Life Building. (Life, I later learned, meant, in this case, life insurance.) And so one morning I slipped out of line at the bus stop, slipped into the Japan Life Building, slipped into the elevator among a throng of gray- and black-suited, briefcase-carrying specimens called in Japan "salaryman," and rode it, gnashing my teeth with impatience as it stopped at every single floor, to the top. There was just me and one other man, everyone else having descended at lower altitudes, and this one other man looked at me curiously, as well he might, for a small boy like me would naturally have appeared very peculiar and out of place there – he seemed about to question me, but I very abruptly turned away and marched down the aisle with an air of someone who knew precisely what he was up to, and I guess he decided it was no business of his, and thus our brief encounter ended.

So there I was on the twelfth and top floor of the Japan Life Building. Well and good – but how to get to the roof? There must be a passage somewhere – or perhaps not; why should there be one? For the benefit of people wanting to kill themselves? Yes, but other people jump from roofs, you read about it in the newspaper from time to time; quite often, in fact... And so I wandered about, seeking the passage, turning the matter over in my mind, my doubts growing, when suddenly I heard, "Stephen-kun!" (Yes, irony upon irony! My parents named me after St. Stephen the martyr.) "What on earth...?" I looked up, in a paroxysm of something like terror, to find myself staring into the astonished face of old white-haired Mr. Saito, a member of my parents' church.

My "paroxysm" was momentary. Mr. Saito's vapid old face, smooth as a girl's and stupid as a sheep's, could still at a glance the wildest emotional flights, whether the emotion in question was fear, despair, or, for that matter, happiness. I mumbled something about coming into the building because I'd got cold standing around waiting for the bus, and taking an elevator out of curiosity... etc. etc.; the sort of thing you mumble in a situation like that. He smiled, patted me on the head, and said I'd better run along or I'd be late for school – which I was, but my explanation was natural enough and the matter ended with a warning from the new teacher not to let it happen again.

———————

I dreamed of my father last night. Have I mentioned my father? I don't remember. To be perfectly honest, I hardly know what I've written. I am filling page after page with I don't know what. "Page," I say, meaning paper. Invented by the Chinese a thousand years ago, it hovers now on the verge of extinction, surviving only so that relics from another age, like me, can compose... whatever it is I am composing. Memoir? Autobiography? "Letter to no one." If I must call it something, maybe that's the best name to give it. Letter to no one. Very likely I will die at this table, pen in hand. Weeks, months will pass; the smell of my rotting corpse will draw attention; the police will be called, they'll break open the door, and there I'll be, what's left of me, grinning horribly, with these yellow sheets of paper scattered about. Will anyone take the trouble to decipher my unsightly scrawl?

My father. His god called him home in rather a peculiar way – or perhaps not. In a *characteristically* peculiar way, I should maybe say. He was en route to a seminar in Tokyo, a seminar of missionaries, and his plane crashed, killing him and, if I remember correctly, 256 others, my mother among them. Strange – I always have to remind myself that my mother too died in the crash. In my imagination she was a victim not of the crash but of my father's death.

In my dream I was sitting with my father in a restaurant, and we were chatting over coffee – as, during what turned out to be the last few months of his life, we often did. I was twenty-three when he died – a graduate student in philosophy, having switched from mathematics. Why? I could have written a book in answer to that question *then*. *Now* I no longer remember, and the anguish the decision cost me, which I *do* remember, seems to me now merely comical, grotesque. In view of my subsequent life, how could it seem otherwise? "Here," I said to my father, "*this* is what it means to believe in God." With that I flung him a copy of Kierkegaard's Fear and Trembling. It is an odd way to present someone with a gift, for that is what it was. The truth is, I loved my father and was ashamed of loving him. To my surprise he read it, and read it with interest. "You see," I said, "the difference between you and Abraham. *He* believed in God *deeply*. *You* believe *shallowly*." His answer shocked me. "Maybe you're right," he said.

In the dream, then, we are sitting in a restaurant and chatting, as had become our wont, only I am speaking the most patent absurdities, the most arrant nonsense, while my father listens intently, nods gravely, murmurs "Yes, yes, I see. Hm." What am I telling him? Of out-of-body experiences, of traveling in time, of meeting God face to face, Who tells me He has a mission for me, for which I must hold myself in readiness. I describe visions that make those of the prophet Ezekiel seem rational. And at first I am ashamed of pulling the wool over my foolish old father's eyes, but the odd thing is that the more I talk – and my inventiveness seems boundless, I never run out of things to say – the fainter grows my consciousness that I am talking nonsense; in short, I come to believe what I'm saying, my tone grows earnest, my hands begin to tremble; by no means in the spirit of raillery I entreat my father's blessing: "Bless me, father, for I know not what awaits me and I am afraid." I woke up trembling with fear. I soon shook it off, but... well, what if I lose my senses? And a strange thought comes to me: that before I do, before darkness closes in, leaving me helpless and alone... shouldn't I get married?

I have never (you will have gathered as much) been married, never thought of marrying. The fact is, the "nonsense" I spoke to my father in my dream has roots in waking reality, and may not be nonsense at all, for the ultimate consequence of my relationship with Miss Small, my brief flirtation with suicide and its abrupt, so to speak, abortion, was a conviction, conceived then and germinating silently over time, that I had been reserved for a special fate, not necessarily relating to the service of God, not necessarily not relating to it either. I mentioned my transfer from mathematics to philosophy. Is there a connection? Between my transfer, I mean, and my growing conviction. I think there is. As a child I was a mathematical prodigy, and had always been drawn to the study of numbers, but here was something that could not be explored in numerical terms. Numbers never preoccupied me exclusively; I was literate too, and used my literacy to good advantage during those teenage years when my classmates were occupied with, shall we say, more rambunctious pursuits. Plato and St. Augustine I knew practically by heart, and the Enlightenment philosophers and the German idealists who followed them. So we needn't look to supernatural motivation to explain the transfer; the ground had been well prepared. But around that time a chance meeting occurred which may have been a decisive influence. The meeting was with none other than Otake – the big bamboo.

———

I didn't recognize him. Even after he hailed me, all affability, laughing at my dismay at hearing my name called in a place where I had every reason to presume I was a perfect stranger; even after he told me who he was – even then I couldn't connect his present appearance – his present *incarnation*, perhaps I should say – with my memory of that grotesque, prematurely mature bully I'd known at the international school.

"Come into my office, we'll have a chat."

I rose and followed him, almost overwhelmed by a feeling I had never known before – a feeling of inferiority. He led me into a spacious, almost cavernous office and closed the door behind us. The floor was carpeted, the walls covered with paintings, like a museum. He ushered me into an armchair of plush leather, lowering his own frame onto the sofa opposite. "Do you know," he said, smiling, "that I came very close to murdering you? Don't laugh" – could he really have seen anything on my face suggestive of laughter? – "it's true; I even bought a knife, a kitchen knife with a 26-centimeter blade; it would've made short work of you; you'd never've seen your twelfth birthday; by now, even to your parents you'd be at most a distant memory. What do you drink?" He rose. There was a liquor cabinet under a painting – brilliant dabs of color representing, I think, chrysanthemums, but I know little of either painting or flowers, so it's just a guess.

"Nothing," I murmured. "Thank you."

He sat down again. "It is rather early in the day. So! Tell me about yourself! What are you up to?"

"I'm studying mathematics at X. University."

"Mathematics! Mathematics. Never my strong suit." He laughed, showing even, white teeth. He was so handsome! It was breathtaking. What wouldn't a man give to have a face like his, an air like his! And if the price of such handsomeness – such beauty – was evil and stupidity? Yes, even at that price, I thought, it's worth it.

"But where does it take you, mathematics? What does it get you?"

"I don't know." If I ever had known, I no longer did; I no longer knew anything. There'd been an ad in the newspaper – the such-and-such furniture company was seeking part-time help; I was seeking a part-time job to help pay my tuition; I answered the ad, and suddenly there I was in that enormous office, face to face with Otake!

"I'm married," he said. "I have two kids – a boy, three, and a girl, eighteen months. It changes your life, you know, having kids."

"Does it?"

"You'll know someday. Forget mathematics. Come work for me. Not *for* me, *with* me. We'll be partners. I need someone like you. And you – though you may not know it yet – need someone like me. This is a growing business. My grandfather built it, my father expanded it, and I'm carrying on the family tradition – building and expanding. It's in the blood. What do you say? Come over for dinner tonight, I'll introduce you to my young and growing family. Did I mention my wife is pregnant?"

After dinner the young and growing family retired to some other region of the vast house, and it was just the two of us. I was not used to drinking, and soon the familiar contours of the physical universe we all live in dissolved. "Glenlivet," I heard him say, and nodded vaguely in reply, hoping vaguely that my incomprehension was not too blatantly obvious. He talked and talked. Had he been so talkative as a boy? I didn't remember and still don't – perhaps one day I will – but his voice was like music; he was happy, and I felt happy listening to him. He loved his wife, loved his children, loved his business; only one thing seemed to disturb him: the fact that I wasn't as happy as he was. But I *could* be, he assured me as he filled my glass; it was so *easy* – he would take me into the business, fix me up with his wife's sister... "Forget mathematics." That was his recurring theme. "Forget mathematics, make babies."

I awoke with a splitting headache and a sour taste in my mouth. Where was I? What had happened? I had thrown up all over the sofa. Otake laughed, his teeth gleaming. I was not to worry – there were plenty more sofas where that came from! It was morning. Sunlight streamed into the room. "I cleaned you up as best I could. Now that you're awake, let me put you to bed." He laughed again, still more delightedly. "Come, partner. We have a nice little bed in a nice little guest room..." I would have fled if I could, but my head was throbbing, throbbing... "Maybe you'd like a hot bath first."

153

Mavrin – where are you? When you come you are a torture to me, you make me cringe, I hate you and long only to be free of you – and yet when you don't come, as tonight... I miss you. Have you abandoned me for good? Has my trial been suspended? Have I been acquitted due to lack of evidence? As to that, I told you there would be no evidence. You didn't believe me. Now you know. But in that case, you must let me out of here. Acquittal means freedom, does it not? Doesn't it? Listen. Never mind the rights and wrongs of the matter. If you let me out, I'll make it worth your while, I'll...

"Naoko-chan!"

"How are you?"

"How long have you been sitting there?"

"Oh, not long. Ten minutes. Can I fix you something? Some hot milk?"

"Yes. Yes, please. Oh, Lord, what a dream! Naoko, tell me..."

"Yes?"

"Tell me the truth. Am I going to live forever, or... or what?"

She smiles. She has such a nice smile. "I wouldn't be surprised."

"But why? Why me?"

"Why not you? Let me get your milk."

"Wait. The milk can wait. First, let's... settle some things. I'm eighty-seven years old, I could die at any time, and before I do..."

"What about living forever?"

"Well, that's just a hypothesis... a... hypothesis!"

"Well? Before you do... what?"

"Two things. First: will you marry me? Wait, don't answer. Second: will you hear my confession? Yes, the time has come for me to confess to you, to you alone..."

"What can you possibly have to confess to me?"

"That I am not the man you think I am. Listen. Do you remember when your house caught fire?"

"Of course! How could I forget?"

"You were a child at the time."

"You don't forget a thing like that."

"You could have been killed. Your whole family could have been killed."

"Yes, it was very lucky my father happened to be awake. He was working in his study and smelled smoke. It was two in the morning. If he'd been asleep..."

"It was I who set that fire, Naoko."

"You!"

"I."

What is the expression taking shape on her face? Horror? Disbelief? "But... no, it's impossible! You're not serious!"

"I have the sort of face that turns everything I say into a kind of joke – that is true. Still..."

"You're ill, you're not well..."

"You're trembling."

"It's chilly. Let me turn on the heater."

"Naoko, listen to me. You thought of me as a family friend, as a kind of uncle. Your father took me into his business, your mother loved me like a sister. None of you had any idea, any *idea*, how I...

155

hated you! Oh, my God, my God how I hated you!"

———————

Her scream hangs in the air. The door through which she fled is still open. Stupid, stupid... that is not at all how I meant to tell her. So many times, so many times I rehearsed it in my mind – even out loud, sometimes, and always I found the words to make her listen to the end – but face to face, I said it all wrong; why, how? Will I ever see her again?

Little Pieces

I live with my sister. Who is convinced she is Marie Antoinette reincarnated. I'm not joking. Neither is she – she really believes it. "Why," I ask her, "would an eighteenth-century French queen be reincarnated as a twenty-first-century Japanese office girl?" She answers, "She wasn't French, she was Austrian." "Yes, I know, but – " "You know nothing, nothing!"

My sister is convinced she has a tragic destiny. Two months ago she refused an offer of marriage from a man who has everything a woman could ask for in a husband – looks, brains, career... And he genuinely loves my sister. I know he does. He told me. Now and then he would take me out for coffee and kind of pour his heart out to me. "I don't think she realizes," he said. "I don't think she understands. I don't understand myself. No woman has ever made me feel the way your sister does. It's... I don't know, it's... *You* believe me, Saya-chan, don't you?" "Yes." "Well, tell her, then. Speak to her for me. Plead my case."

Which I was only too happy to do. "Don't you see he loves you?" I said. "Yes," she said, "I know." "Well?" "You're too young to understand." "Let's pretend I'm not," I said; "let's pretend for once that I'm a normal human being and that you can talk to me, you know, more or less normally. Woman to woman, so to speak."

"If I marry him, he'll murder me."

"Murder you!"

"Yes, murder me! *You* look at him and see a handsome face, a friendly smile! *I* look at him and see..."

"Well? You look at him and see what?"

"What he really is!"

With that, in tears, she flung herself out of the kitchen and into her bedroom, slamming the door behind her.

I think my sister is emotionally disturbed. I wish there was something I could do for her. But the truth is I simply don't know what to do. I'm at a loss. Sometimes I feel her disturbance infecting me. Just last night I woke up suddenly. It was pitch dark. I heard a noise, like the creaking of a floorboard, and I thought, "My sister's going to murder me!" I was paralyzed with terror. After a time I was able to master my fear, convince myself I was being ridiculous, but it was long before I could get back to sleep, and now, sipping my morning tea, I feel just awful.

"I think I'll call in sick today," I say to my sister.

"Oh?"

"I don't feel well. I couldn't sleep last night."

"Funny, neither could I."

I have to talk to somebody, and there's only one person I can think of who might understand and advise me – my sister's boyfriend, or ex-boyfriend, the man she refused to marry. There would be nothing strange in my calling him. They used to sometimes take me with them when they went to a movie or out to dinner or something, and he and I seemed to have a natural affinity for one another. I don't mean there was anything *romantic* between us – oh, no! But I did enjoy his company, and he enjoyed mine, or seemed to, and sometimes we even went out just the two of us, with my sister's knowledge and permission, sometimes even her encouragement. He was sort of like an older brother to me, and at times I think I was sort of like an older sister to him. Does he know, I wonder, the strange fancies my sister is subject to? He can hardly *not* know them, they are so much a part of her. But why would so *normal* a man, one so clearly marked out for success of every kind, have fallen so deeply in love with someone so... disturbed? "Disturbed" – it's the only word I can think of. I really don't know what is at the root of my sister's trouble.

———

My supervisor is not pleased to hear from me. I am a cashier at the Rally supermarket on Route 5, a ten-minute walk from our apartment. "I have never called in sick before," I remind her, and she grants that in the two years I have worked there I have been steady and dependable – but that, she hastens to add, is hardly an excuse for dereliction now. Dereliction! "I am sick and can't work today," I say with quiet finality. "If that's a firing offense, fire me." I snap the phone shut, not giving her a chance to reply.

What would turn a pretty young woman like her into such a bitch? I knew her before she became a supervisor; she was really nice. Well, I suppose she has her problems like everyone else. Now she has to find someone to replace me, failing which she may even have to fill in for me herself.

My sister's gone to her office, the apartment is empty and quiet, I can go back to bed now and get some sleep. Strange, though – I no longer feel sleepy, or even tired. Shall I call back and say I can work after all? No, I'd only look foolish.

Does she *really* think she's Marie Antoinette? Does she *really* think Kenichi will murder her? For the first time the thought occurs to me that she's teasing me, having a laugh at my expense. She's twenty-seven, I'm twenty, and when we were growing up her greatest pleasure in life was to bait me, make a fool of me. Once when I was nine and she sixteen she told me that the world would explode on my tenth birthday, and everything, everything would cease to exist. "Where will we go?" I asked her. "You don't understand," she said. "We won't go anywhere. We will cease to be." "You mean we'll die?" "No, it's not the same as dying because when a person dies the world remains as it was, but on your birthday *everything* will cease to be." "Why on my birthday?"

"Because that's what's fated." And so on. Of course I didn't believe her, but on the other hand I didn't *dis*believe her either, and as my birthday approached my trepidation grew to the point where it was almost unbearable. I said nothing of this to her, and she herself never mentioned it again... I could cite numerous other examples; it's the price you pay for growing up in the shadow of someone so much older. I would have thought that by now she'd put such childish games behind her, but maybe to her I'm still just a little kid whose unfailing credulity is an irresistible temptation. Maybe I should move out, get my own place. Maybe then she'd forget about being Marie Antoinette, marry Kenichi, and get on with her life. Yes, maybe that's what I'll do.

———————

The whole day stretches before me, solitary and free. What shall I do? It's a beautiful crisp fall morning; I could go for a walk. Or I could read. There are plenty of books in the apartment. My sister's books. Her bedroom is almost a library, it's so full of books. You almost never see her without a book in her hand. What she gets from all her reading I don't know. She is forever after me to follow her example. Why don't I read this, supposing I read that? I should enrich my mind, develop my thinking powers. Why – so I can go mad, like her? "One genius in the family is enough," I tell her. Yes, it really is time I crawled out from under my sister's shadow and... Well, maybe that's what I'll do today! Find a place to live, a nice quiet little apartment, a room of my own.

A room of my own. I can almost see it – a white room, bathed in sunlight, lace curtains fluttering in the breeze. All I have to do is find it and it's mine! Very well then. I slip on my jacket, it's apt to be a bit chilly at this time of year... What else do I need? Key, wallet, cell phone... Good! Goodbye!

————

II

Of all the stupid, idiotic predicaments! I finally get the older sister off my back, and now the younger one is dogging me! Here's *another* message from her on my cell phone. What should I do – ignore her? That's what I've *been* doing, but she doesn't seem to get the point. All right then, I'll call her back, and tell her in no uncertain terms... But that's the trouble. I *can't* tell her "in no uncertain terms." She's such a sad, lonely, ugly, pathetic little thing; stupid into the bargain; but so kind, so gentle, I can't bear to hurt her!

"Sayaka? It's Ken. Listen – "

"Ken-chan!"

"Yes. Is something wrong?"

"Oh... it's my sister. I'm so worried about her, I wish I knew... wish I understood..."

"Sayaka, listen to me. Your sister and I are no longer... we broke up, you see."

"Then it's... it's final? It's all over?"

"Yes, dear, it's over. I'm sorry."

"I see."

She is silent, and I don't know what to say. I can imagine what a fool I look like to my department head, Mr. Iinami, who has come over to my desk and is squinting at me in some surprise. "Are you on the phone?" he inquires in a voice barely above a whisper, to minimize his intrusion if it is one.

I raise a finger to indicate I'll be with him in a minute and say into the phone, "Sayaka, I have to go now, I'm at work, you see, and my boss – "

"Couldn't you meet me for lunch? I'm downtown."

"Downtown? What are you doing downtown?"

"For a quick cup of tea, if not for lunch. You see, I... I so need to talk to someone... someone older, more experienced..."

"All right, we'll have lunch. What time is it now? Ten past eleven. Do you know the Nakamuraya sushi shop, across the street from the Clock Tower? Meet me there at one."

Mr. Iinami shakes his head and smiles. "Sayaka? Yesterday it was Mayu."

"It still is Mayu. Sayaka is the kid sister of someone I broke up with two months ago. I was... kind of an older brother to her, I guess, and... well, she seems to need someone like me. What she *really* needs is a good psychiatrist, but I'm not sure I know how to get her to see one."

"Are you sure she isn't in love with you?"

163

"The thought has crossed my mind."
"Let her down gently, Ozawa-kun."
"As gently as I can."

This is strange... she isn't here. It's ten past one... It's not like her to be late for a meeting with me. Even if I arrive early, I always find her waiting for me. Can something have happened to her? Ridiculous – what can have happened? Nothing ever does happen to her, poor child. That's probably the root of what ails her. Or maybe it's because of what ails her that nothing ever happens to her. Anyway. Listen, my dear, I'm in the middle of a working day, I can't stand here all day waiting for you. We said one o'clock. Well, I'll give you five more minutes, and then, you'll have to excuse me, I must be off.

Strange, strange. I can't get it out of my mind, though I really do have other things to think about. Why didn't she show up? Or at least call? Come to think of it, why didn't I call her? I'm lying to myself if I say it didn't occur to me. Of course it did – and yet I didn't call. I used her not showing up as an excuse to wash my hands of her, and now I feel guilty – but why? She stood me up, not the other way around, and if I'm secretly relieved to have been let off the hook, as I admit I am, where's the sin? Where's the crime? She's the kid sister of an ex-girlfriend, which is as good as saying she's nothing to me. If she has an adolescent crush on me, that's her problem – isn't it? Still, maybe I should at least dial her number, to make sure she's not in trouble or something...

"Ozawa-kun!" Iinami-san. "Come, let's go out for a beer. Unless, of course, Mayu-san's waiting for you."

"She is, as a matter of fact."

"Well, off you go then! I can't afford to pay you any more overtime this month."

———

Actually, Mayu is not waiting for me. Mayu is working tonight - not where she thinks I think she's working, which is to say at her office, but where I happened to find out she is really working, which is to say... good God, how complicated life is in the twenty-first century! Is "complicated" even the word? Father Matsui, bless him - he's the priest at my church; yes, I am a Catholic, I was baptized at fifteen, and how many times since then I have fallen away from the church and returned to it and fallen away again I simply do not know anymore, I've lost count - Father Matsui, my true friend and wise counselor over the years, thinks the end of the world is near, very near, and quotes the Book of Revelation to prove it! You laugh, but I'll tell you frankly, he makes a lot more sense to me than the so-called realists who pin their faith on science and economics and mock the notion of salvation through divine grace. Don't get me wrong: I know their arguments as well as they do, I'm an economist myself, I can mock as bitingly as they

165

can. But more and more my mockery leaves a bitter taste in my mouth. Who am I fooling?

No, but... shall I tell you what I think? It is not the *end* of the world we're living through, not the end, but the beginning. It's not that God created the world – God *is creating* the world! Yes, yes. I see it now: this is the Creation we're living through. These are the six days. Or perhaps the sixth day. Or perhaps the first. Would Father Matsui be in his office now, I wonder? I must... I must have a talk with him! Oh, Father, please, please be in your office!

———

Where am I? It is strange. I was born in this city, grew up here, have never lived anywhere else – how is it I get lost in it so easily? I have no sense of direction, that's the trouble.

Anyway... anyway! I found my apartment. I recognized it as soon as the man, the agent, ushered me inside. "Yes, this is the place," I said. The agent was surprised. This was only the first of several apartments he'd planned to show me, and his quick success didn't seem to please him.

"What do you mean, 'this is the place'?" he asked.

"Why, this is the place, I saw it in my dream: a white room bathed in sunlight, lace curtains fluttering in the breeze... Last night I dreamed of this very room. Yes, it was this room, this room and no other. Can I move in today?"

"Well, you'll need someone to act as a guarantor. Your father, perhaps?"

"My parents are dead."

"Well..."

"There's only my elder sister," I said. "I'm living with her now."

"Well, that's fine then. Bring your sister to our office, and as soon as the paperwork is done you can move in."

"She works during the week. Will Saturday be all right?"

"Any day except Sunday. Can I drop you somewhere?"

"No, thank you. Would it be possible, do you think... could I just... sit here for a few minutes? Alone?"

"Sit here? But there's nothing to sit on!"

"I'll sit on the floor. Please, I want to so much."

"I'm afraid I... I have to lock up, you see."
"Why? There's nothing to steal, is there?"

"No, that's true. Still..."

"I'll tell you what. You had other places to show me; you were planning to spend a lot more time with me, weren't you? You didn't expect to wrap up our business nearly so quickly. Just let me sit here quietly for an hour, and then come back for me and I'll leave with you. Or maybe I'll even be gone before you come back. Would that be all right?"

"Well, it's highly irregular, but... all right. One hour."

"One hour. Really, you're so kind. I can't thank you enough. And I'll bring my sister to your office on Saturday. Saturday morning."

———

I think... I think I know this park. It looks familiar. That little stream, with the little wooden bridge over it. Didn't my father take me here when I was little? I was five when Father died. Mother told me that he used to take me out every Sunday morning, for a drive or for a walk, just the two of us. My sister had ballet on Sunday morning, and Father and I... "Where did he take me?" I remember asking my mother. "I don't know, dear," she said. Could it have been here? I'm sure I haven't been here recently. It's quite far from anywhere I ever go. But... surely I've stood on this bridge before? This railing – didn't Father lift me up and sit me on it? Could I be mistaken? Of course I could be – it could have been some other bridge, some other railing, or maybe I'm imagining the whole scene... But then... why did this feeling of having been here before suddenly hit me? I've never had it before... I wonder if my sister would know. It's not likely, if my mother didn't. Still, I'll ask her. Funny: she must remember Father so much more clearly than I do. I hardly remember him at all. And it's funny that we never speak of him – never. You'd think the subject would come up, in the course of conversation, but it never does. Hm. If only I had a better sense of direction! I'll have to stop somebody and ask the way to the subway station – and I so hate to do that!

"Ozawa-san! Come in, come in. What a surprise."

"I'm sorry, Father, I should have called."

"Nonsense, nonsense!"

Father Matsui was once a circus clown, and there are times when, even in his cassock, he looks more like a clown than a priest. He's a dwarfish little man, with a slight hump on his back and a perpetual smile on his ruddy face that at times, truth to tell, looks rather foolish. In fact there's little about his exterior that commands respect. His head, with its bald patches and scattered clumps of gray hair seeming to form a different pattern every time you see him, is the shape of a soccer ball and seems to sit directly on his shoulders, so insignificant is his neck. I remember once he said to me, very early in our acquaintance, "How would they hang me if I ever came up for capital punishment?" With me at a loss for a reply, he promptly added, "I'd better keep my nose clean, eh? So as not to embarrass the state!"

"Sit down," he says, "let me get you some tea."

"Father, I've come for your blessing."

"Oh?"

"Bless me, Father, for I have... decided to disappear. To vanish without a word to anyone.

You are the last person I will see as my present self. When I leave this church it will be as a nameless, penniless, homeless, aimless vagrant. I will spend my days walking, my evenings begging, my nights sleeping in whatever shelter the proceeds of my begging can procure for me..."

"And why this... this..."

"I seem to hear the voice of God telling me this is what I must do."

"If that's a joke, my son, it's not funny, and in fact – "

" – would be blasphemous. I know. No, I'm not joking. It is the service God demands of me. Each of us is called to serve Him in a different way – you as priest, me as... what? Up-and-coming executive at Nomura Securities? Lover of Mayu, who two nights a week sells herself to... well, to people like me..."

"Sells herself?"

"Sells herself. The old-fashioned word for it is whore. One of my friends... one of my colleagues, I should say (I have no friends), met her at an establishment known in the industry as a soapland. You are familiar with such establishments, Father?"

"I've heard of them, certainly."

"Well, she works in one two nights a week – telling *me* she works late. Which of course she does, so I can't accuse her of lying. I don't accuse her of anything. I only see that... that my present way of life is mistaken, that I must... well, as I said..."

"Shouldn't you at least talk to Mayu-san first? Aren't you too quick to think the worst of her? For all you know, it might be a case of mistaken identity."

"Oh no, Father, it's not mistaken identity, and I am by no means quick to think the worst of her. On the contrary, I was very slow. Before I stationed myself outside the club and with my own eyes saw her enter – and it was long before I could even bring myself to do that – I too assumed it was a case of mistaken identity."

"My son – "

"No, Father, I have made up my mind. If this isn't a sign from God, there is no such thing. Your blessing, Father. I ask, I implore your blessing."

"My blessing you have, no matter what you do. But... mayn't we talk a little longer?"

"Oh, certainly, Father, as long as you like. As long as you can endure my company."

"And you will permit me to be perfectly frank with you?"

"Perfectly."

"I don't mean to pry, but before you started seeing Mayu there was another girl, another woman."

"Yes."

"Her name was...?"

"Tomoko."

"Tomoko. And before Tomoko, I think..."

"I see what you're getting at. 'Let he who is without sin cast the first stone.' My own life is far from blameless. All the more reason – "

"All the more reason, I should think, to stop and reflect before taking a step that, whatever you might say to the contrary, is being taken in the spirit of anger and resentment."

"I say nothing to the contrary. Anger and resentment – yes, and to spare. Just this afternoon I was sitting at my desk and asking myself, could I murder Mayu? Would I be capable of it? And my tentative conclusion – tentative because after all, how well do we really know ourselves? – my tentative conclusion is yes, I could. In today's evening paper there's a story about a deranged man who stabbed a woman, a complete stranger, stabbed her to death in the street with a fruit knife. He'd bought the knife at a hardware store half an hour before, with the express intention of using it to stab someone. I happened to read the story on the subway here, and the first thought that came into my head was, 'Maybe I'll buy a fruit knife.' So seriously, Father, isn't it better for me to go?"

"My son..." We look at each other in silence for a time, and when at last he breaks the silence it's to say, "We will do the only thing I know how to do in a crisis. We will kneel down and pray. And when we rise from our knees, with God's grace you will know what to do. And, with God's grace, you will do it."

"Do you really believe that, Father?"

"Oh yes, my son. Yes. I really believe that. Would I have become a priest if I didn't? Wouldn't I still be a clown? It's a good life, you know, a clown's..."

III

"Tomoko, it's me."
Silence.
"It's Ken."
Silence.
"May I come in?"
The door does not open.
"Please, Tomoko. I must speak to you. You don't..." One feels foolish, talking like this into an intercom. "You don't know what is going on in my soul."

"No, I don't! And I don't want to! I am terrified, terrified of what goes on in your soul!"

"Terrified?" This is a surprise. "Why?"

"Why don't you just... go away!"

"I will, of course, if you want me to." Thank heaven there is no one on the stairs. "You have every reason to... well, to hate me. But..." I try a new tack. "Is Sayaka home?"

"What do you want with her?"

"What do I want with her? Nothing, I... Tomoko, please, I can't talk here, there's someone coming."

There is, in fact, suddenly, the sound of footsteps coming somewhat hurriedly up the stairs. Father Matsui would surely see the hand of Providence at work, for the newcomer is none other than Sayaka. "Ken-chan!"

"Sayaka! You were supposed to meet me this afternoon. I was worried."

"I... I'm sorry, I... But come in. Isn't my sister home?"

"She is, but she won't let me in."

"What's the matter with her?"

Sayaka takes her key from her handbag and opens the door.

"Where were you?" Tomoko pounces on Sayaka quite as if I weren't here. "I was worried sick!"

"Worried sick about what? I don't have the right to go out any more? You keep me here like a prisoner in a cage. I'm sick of it. I found my own apartment. I'm moving out."

"You're what?"

"Moving out. And if you won't sign as my guarantor, I'll ask Ken-chan. I'm going to take a bath."

With that she moves past us down the hallway.

Tomoko turns to me. Her eyes are wide; there is a look of something like fear in them. She takes a step back, then another. She reminds me of something. For a moment I can't quite grasp what it is. Then it comes to me: the woman in Munch's painting, The Scream. But no sooner has this struck me than her expression changes. What is it welling up behind her eyes – laughter? Yes – wild, mocking laughter! But that too passes almost as soon as I perceive it. Now there is no laughter, no mockery, only a smile, just an ordinary smile. "Well, since you're here," she says, "you may as well stay for dinner. What is it you 'must speak to me' about?"

"About – "

"Wait a minute. Sayaka!" she suddenly calls out. "Sayaka!"

Sayaka, having disappeared into the kitchen, now reappears at the opposite end of the long hallway. Declining to come closer, she stands, mute and expressionless, waiting to hear what her sister wants.

"What's this about moving out? What's this about a guarantor?"

"I'm twenty years old. I want to be on my own. I found an apartment. It's just like one I saw in a dream. I recognized it immediately. I told the man I'd take it, but he said I need a guarantor. It's near Makomanai Park. Did Father ever take me to Makomanai Park? As I was walking there this afternoon, I seemed to remember – "

"Father!"

"Yes, Father. Is there some reason we never mention him? It's like there's some taboo or something."

"You want to move out? Is that the way you show your gratitude to me, after all I've – "

"Gratitude!"

"After all I've done for you, all I've sacrificed?"

Sayaka now approaches us, walking slowly. About half way to us she stops again. She stands in the middle of the hall, her left shoulder resting lightly against the wall, regarding us in silence. No one speaks. Why did I come? I'm no longer sure. To say goodbye? To beg forgiveness? To propose marriage? I hear Sayaka say, calmly, almost indifferently, "You're mad, Sister. Are you aware of that? You're mad." She turns around and starts to walk away, but Tomoko calls out, "Wait!", and she stops.

"Let's all go into the living room," says Tomoko. "I have something to say to you. And when I've said it, you can judge whether I'm mad or not."

———

Their "living room" is a purely Japanese-style room – tatami floor, cushions instead of chairs, and an alcove in which, over an old-fashioned lantern-like lamp, hung a scroll. I have always been drawn to that scroll. I know little of such things, and have no idea as to its artistic value – it may be trash for all I know. It illustrates a famous poem by the haiku master Basho: "Crow on a withered branch, autumn eve." That's exactly what it shows, and that's all it shows. Tomoko and I found it one day in a dusty little antique shop we happened to wander into. It was very early in our relationship. We looked at it without comment, and then left the shop. The next day I went back and bought it. On our next date I made her a present of it. That's the history of the scroll in Tomoko's "living room."

We have scarcely seated ourselves on the cushions arranged round the low table that is the room's only furniture before Tomoko begins. She sits facing Sayaka, and speaks exclusively to her. I may as well not be there. In fact, I have the odd, eerie feeling that I'm not – that I left the church and, just as I told Father Matsui I would, vanished. I see and hear everything that goes on, but any sense of my being *present* at the scene is utterly lacking.

"Let me tell you first of all," says Tomoko, speaking quietly and unemotionally, almost monotonously, "that the man you call 'Father' is my father but not yours. We are not sisters. We are nothing to each other. You came into this family when you were four years old. Your father murdered your mother. He stabbed her to death with a bread knife and stuffed her corpse into the trunk of his car. This happened in Tokyo. He then fled with you to Narita Airport, and abandoned you there. You were barely three years old. You were found wandering lost and crying in the airport concourse, clutching a stuffed animal. I'll show you the newspaper clippings; I still have them. The police were called, and you were taken to an orphanage. Your father, meanwhile, had flown to Los Angeles, where some weeks later he was arrested. He was sent back to Japan, tried, and sentenced to life in prison. If he is alive he is still there – unless he's been paroled for good behavior or something, which is possible for all I know. As to how you came into this family and became my 'sister' – "

"Tomoko, stop!" That was my voice; I heard it distinctly, but no one else seemed to. Neither Tomoko nor Sayaka pay me the slightest attention.

Michael Hoffman

Sayaka's eyes are fixed on her sister. What is going on in her mind? Her face reveals nothing – but then, Sayaka's face scarcely ever does, a thought that strikes me just now for the first time. Sayaka's face does not register emotion. Could it be paralyzed in some way? Would that account for the odd cast of her features?

"As to how you came into this family and became my 'sister,' my parents had long believed it wasn't healthy for a girl to grow up an only child; they wanted another one, but my mother had had a hysterectomy shortly after I was born, so adoption was the only way. For years they couldn't make up their minds. Then your story hit the papers. My father showed the story to my mother and said, 'Here she is, here's our child.' That's what my mother told me years later. She never told me how she responded to that – whether in astonishment she asked him what on earth he meant, or whether she simply understood him and agreed without any explanation being necessary. Be that as it may, they filed the necessary applications, underwent the necessary tests – "

Without a word Sayaka rises to her feet and walks out of the room. There is no hurried abruptness in her movements, no agitation; she moves like someone who, after sitting in one place for a long time, simply feels like getting up. A moment later we hear her bedroom door close softly. Then we hear nothing.

Tomoko turns to me. "I'll see about dinner," she says, and she too stands up.

178

Left alone, I sit gazing up at the crow on the withered branch. I don't know how long I sit there, in motionless silence, thinking nothing. Then a faint sound from the kitchen – the sound of meat sizzling on a fry pan – startles me out of my reverie. I stand up and walk past the kitchen, where through the doorway I see Tomoko, her back to me, busy at the stove. At Sayaka's bedroom door I hesitate, then knock gently. No answer. "Sayaka," I call, for some reason not daring to raise my voice much above a whisper. "Sayaka. It's me. May I come in?" Still no answer. Perhaps she hasn't heard me. I turn the doorknob. Is it locked? No. I only meant to open it a crack, but it seems to swing open of itself, revealing a brilliantly lit room – brilliant at least in comparison to the dim lamplight of the living room. Sayaka sits cross-legged on the futon in the middle of the floor. Her eyes seem to have been fixed even before I enter precisely on the space that my face now occupies, so she doesn't have to move a muscle to confront me.

"May I come in?"

"Of course."

There is only one chair in the room – a little white chair that is evidently of a set with the little white desk. I sit down on it, feeling foolish as only a grown man sitting in a child's chair can. Sayaka sees my discomfort and, patting the space beside her on the futon, says, "Sit here.

"Do you think," I say, "we could turn off the overhead light and turn on this desk lamp instead?"

"Is it too bright?"

"Yes, I rather think it is."

"I like bright lights. When I was little I was afraid of the dark."

"And now?"

"Now not so much."

"Well, could I... Do you mind?" I switch on the lamp, stand up, cross over to the light switch by the door, and turn off the overhead fluorescent light. "There, that's better, don't you think?"

"Sit here," she says again. "That chair's too small for you."

"Yes, all right. Thank you. Saya-chan..."

"I've decided to quit my job."

"Yes?"

"You want to hear something funny? Wait." She stands up, crosses over to the desk, and from one of the drawers draws out a name card, which she hands me. "Three days ago a rather nice-looking young man – not as nice-looking as you, but still – said to me as I was ringing up his purchases, speaking very low so no one else could hear, 'Listen, I know what you're going through, I can read the expression on your face, I've had it on my own face often enough! I can help you. Give me a call.' And he handed me his card."

"Atsushi Nakajima. Wasn't there a writer of that name?"

"I don't know. My sister's the one who knows about writers. Me, I..."

"What expression would he have seen on your face?"

"I don't know! I was so taken by surprise, I just stared at him, and before I knew it he was gone. Let's call and ask him."

"No, Saya, let's not. There are strange people about nowadays. It's wisest not to encourage them."

"Oh please, Ken-chan, call him."

"Me!"

"If I call, it's maybe asking for trouble. But you... you have a voice that inspires confidence and at the same time..."

"At the same time what?"

"Sends a warning. You're a man of the world. You know your way around. If he has anything nasty in mind, hearing your voice will make him think twice. You can tell him you're my father or something."

"What's this about quitting your job?"

"Well, I'm not going to be a supermarket cashier forever, am I?"

"No, certainly not. What do you have in mind?"

"Maybe I'll go back to school and study Greek drama."

"Oh?"

"No, I'm joking. In high school our drama club performed Antigone."

"Hm."

"What do you think I should do?"

"Really, I... I don't know what to tell you."

"I wish you'd tell me something!"

"Well, going back to school would be a good start. Without an education there's not much – "

"You know what I'd really like to do?"

"What?"

"Start my own business."

"That's interesting. What kind of business?"

"Or better still, marry a rich, rich businessman. Is it possible a rich businessman would want me for a wife? I wouldn't be in his way. I wouldn't mind, you know, if he had affairs with other women."

"You wouldn't? You'd be a very unusual wife, in that case."

"I wouldn't mind at all. I'd even like it. I'd wait up for him no matter how late he came home, and I'd listen while he told me all about the woman he'd just slept with."

"I don't know whether to take you seriously or not."

"Anyway, will you be my guarantor for the apartment I want to rent? I don't want to be under my sister's thumb any more."

"You'd rather be under my thumb?"

"Well, yes, if it comes to that. But you'd treat it as what it is, a mere formality. My sister would make a big deal out of it. One more responsibility on her already over-burdened shoulders! She might even refuse, saying I'm not fit to live on my own. I don't want to be dependent on her consent. I want to say to her, 'Sister, I'm moving out.' Not, 'Sister, is it all right if I move out? Will you sign the papers showing you approve?'"

"Well... but you see, Saya-chan, I may be going away... far away... for a long time. I've been..."

"Dinner's burnt!"

Sayaka and I look at one another. A moment later Tomoko appears in the doorway. "I burned the dinner," she says. "It's a charred mess. I don't know what happened. My thoughts distracted me. I was thinking about something, and suddenly..." Her eyes filled with tears.

"Let's go out for dinner," says Sayaka. "Ken-chan will treat us."

"You two go. I don't want any dinner."

"Nonsense," I say. "Sayaka's right. My treat – and I know just the restaurant to take you to! We'll have a feast!"

IV

"Let's order another bottle," says Sayaka.

"Are you sure?"

"This is the first time I've ever been drunk!"

"And it feels good?"

"Yes! Wonderful!"

"Well, let me give you the benefit of my long experience and let you in on a little secret. The way you feel right now is the very best feeling wine can give. If we order another bottle you'll get depressed, then maybe sick."

"Waiter!"

The waiter who happens to be passing with a tray of empty plates is not ours, but he comes over anyway.

"Another bottle of... this stuff! What is it, Ken-chan?"

"Burgundy."

"It's my first time, I know nothing about wine!"

The waiter smiles thinly, nods vaguely and proceeds on his way.

"Well, I guess you'll just have to find out for yourself," I hear myself murmur. The truth is, I'm rather affected myself. I've never been much of a drinker.

"Tell me, Ken-chan... Is what my sister said true?"

"I don't know. What did she say?"

"About... you know, the... about my father and... and..."

"I don't know. It sounds pretty improbable."

"But you know... I'll tell you something strange! As she was speaking, I seemed to... I don't know, I felt these... these memories coming back."

"What memories?"

"Of being alone and terrified in a vast, vast throng..."

Our waiter comes with our wine. He uncorks it with all the gusto of a magician pulling a rabbit out of a hat, does a comic little pirouette, and fills our glasses. Sayaka laughs. The waiter bows.

"To life!" cries Sayaka, raising her glass.

"Sh, keep your voice down." Heads are turning in our direction.

"To life!" she cries again, louder. "Don't talk to me as if I'm a child. Don't you dare!"

"All right, but if we make a disturbance they'll call the police and have us turned out, so let's behave ourselves."

"You're no fun. I wish my sister was here."

"Is she fun?"

"Do you know that she was afraid you would murder her?"

"Afraid I'd murder her!"

"Sh! Keep your voice down!" She giggles.

"What are you talking about?"

"My sister is mad, Ken. Don't you know that? Shall I tell you a thought that occurs to me? A secret, secret thought? It's that right now, right this very instant, she's slitting her wrist in the bath, and I'll get home and find – "

"Sayaka, please!"

" – find her corpse floating in blood. It's all very well for you to say 'Sayaka please' – but you don't know her! You can't imagine..."

"What can't I imagine?"

"Right now, right this very minute, I feel a stabbing pain in my left wrist. If what she said is true she's not my sister, but we still grew up together, nothing can change that, and we're very close, there's a kind of... bond between us. Do you have brothers and sisters, Ken-chan?"

"No, I'm an only child."

"Then you don't know. There's a kind of... a kind of bond... Oh, my head is spinning!"

"You see, I was right. Now you'll get depressed, and – "

"No! I feel wonderful! Fill my glass. Fill it, I said! Because when you feel this wonderful, there's only one thing you want, one thing you want, and that is... to feel more wonderful! Oh, Ken... Do you know what? I think I love you! For the first time in my life I am drunk and in love!"

———

It's 3 a.m. and she's still not home. Should I call the police? They'll laugh at me; they'll say I'm hysterical. If we had to open an investigation for everyone who stayed out late, they'll say, we'd really have our hands full! Take a sleeping pill and go to sleep. You'll wake up in the morning, your sister will be home safe and sound, you'll see.

Yes, maybe I will take a sleeping pill. I should have done it hours ago. If I take one now I won't be able to wake up on time. On time, on time! I spend my whole life being on time! Good old Tomoko, never late, always on time, someone you can really count on!

What's that – my phone? Good heavens, yes, it is my phone! At three o'clock in the morning! It must be her – who else? Only... I'm so exhausted, so disoriented – where *is* my phone? But what's the matter with me? It's right here in my hand, I was fiddling with it the whole time I was thinking of calling the police. "Hello!"

"Hello, is this Tomoko-san?"

It's not Saya. "Who is this?"

"You don't know me. My name is Mayu Yamazaki, I apologize for calling at this hour, forgive me for waking you..."

"You didn't wake me. Mayu Yamazaki?"

"I'm a... I'm a friend of Kenichi-san's... Tomoko-san? Are you there?"

"Yes... yes. A friend of Kenichi-san's. He's very popular. He has a great many friends, a great many – probably a lot more than either of us knows. There are people like that, you know. They have a certain charm, a certain... well, maybe it's charisma. They flash you a smile, and before you know it you're in love. Forgive me, I'm incoherent. I'm dead tired, I can't see straight, let alone think. Anyway, Ken-chan is one of those."

"Yes, he's very attractive. Is he with you?"

"With me? No. With my younger sister. They went out for dinner and she's not back yet."

"Your younger sister!"

"How do you happen to have my phone number, by the way?"

"It was on Kenichi-san's cell phone. I – "

"You made a note of it, in case of emergency. I understand. Well, he's not here."

"If you hate me, I understand, but please – "

"Hate you! Why should I hate you?" Who is this woman? What does she want from me?

"You won't hang up on me?"

"If I hang up on you, it won't be because I hate you but because I am very tired and must get some sleep. I have to work tomorrow... today, I mean."

"I would very much like for us to become better acquainted."

It is on the tip of my tongue to ask why, but something holds me back – my breeding? My early instruction in etiquette and good manners? "Yes, by all means," I hear myself say.

"What time do you finish work?"

"Usually at five, but sometimes – "

"There's overtime. I understand. I am in the same position myself. Suppose, then, we meet tomorrow... today... at seven. We can have dinner."

"Dinner?" I am stupid with fatigue – maybe also with stupidity, I don't know.

"My treat. Please, don't refuse me. I do so much want – "

"Yes, all right, dinner."

"Where is your office?"

"Right downtown. In the Nippon Life Building."

"The Nippon Life Building! My office is in the Nippon Life Building too! What's your company?"

"The Japan Travel Bureau."

"You're a travel agent?"

"Yes."

"It's on the ground floor, I know it well. I arrange my business trips with JTB. We must have seen each other, maybe even spoken to each other. I had a funny feeling right from the start that your voice sounded familiar. All right, I'll be at your office at seven sharp. Agreed?"

"Yes." Anything to end this conversation so that I can go to bed and lose consciousness. I want so, so badly to lose consciousness!

"One more thing."

"What?"

"I know a man who, for a fee, will kill anyone, no questions asked. But we'll talk about that tomorrow. Today, rather. This evening. I've kept you too long already. I'm sorry. Goodnight, Tomoko-san."

"Yes, thank you," I mumble idiotically. I am already asleep, already unconscious.

"This is a new life, Saya-chan. Look at that sun! Look! Is that the same sun we woke up to yesterday morning? It is not. Nor are we the same. Oh, Saya-chan, to think... to think..."

"Why are you crying?"

"Let it be. Let me cry. These tears I am not ashamed of, not ashamed to have you see. Saya... listen to me, Saya. Listen."

"Well? I'm listening!"

"Do you feel it too, Saya? That we are not the same people we were yesterday, that that sun, this earth, everything, everything has been transformed? Do you feel it, Saya? Only tell me you feel it too, and I'll... I'll..."

"I do, I do feel it! Oh, Ken..."

"Transformed out of recognition! You call me Ken and I call you Saya, but that's just habit, that's just convention. Ken and Saya is who we *were* – not who we *are*. We'll have to begin our new life by taking new names."

"What new names?"

"We'll see. We'll know when the time comes. Listen. First we'll go to Father Matsui and ask his blessing. Then – "

"Who's Father Matsui?"

"The priest at my church. My friend and guardian angel."

"You belong to a church? You're a Christian?"

"I *was* a Christian. *Ken* was a Christian. *I* am nothing. You are nothing. We have no past, or rather... our past was on another planet, in another universe."

"Yes, another universe."

"You see? You understand me. You, only you – "

"I understand nothing, nor want to understand anything, but I love what you are saying, and... and the way you're saying it. Go on. Tell me more."

"We'll go to Father Matsui and ask his blessing, and then we will find a place to raise our child – "

"Our child!"

"Didn't you feel it, Saya? Didn't you feel that we conceived a child? I felt it so... so powerfully. Never, never have I felt anything like that before! Oh, Saya, you mustn't... you're still thinking in terms of the old universe, the old ways. Everything, everything has been transformed!"

"Teach me! Teach me the new and transformed universe. How will we live? Will we have to work? Do we need money in this new universe, or do we simply reach out and take whatever we need?"

"At first, certainly, we will need money, but no more than we already have. And then... but surely you're not afraid of poverty?"

"I am afraid of nothing."

V

"May I speak to you for a moment?"

I look up from my drink, none too affably. I don't come here for conversation. I come here to be alone. Not that there's any company to run away from at home, but when I get tired of sitting alone in my apartment I come here, to sit alone among people, as it were. For me, that's socializing.

Who am I? A professor, a learned man. Learned in what? Ancient history, the more ancient the better. That's what I teach, the first civilizations. Sumer. Egypt. Perhaps you've read my commentary on the Epic of Gilgamesh, or my study of the Book of Genesis chapters relating to the patriarch Abraham. The latter, at least, is still in print.

"Well? What do you want to speak to me about?" Probably a former student, charmed at the prospect of renewing our acquaintance. In which case I suppose I should be a little more cordial. Or maybe the expression on my face is more cordial than I know, because the man pulls up a chair and sits down, quite as if I'd invited him to.

"About life," he says.

He is, I would guess, about thirty-five, which is to say nearly half my age. Squint though I do at his face, I see nothing familiar in it. He is the sort of man you characterize at a glance – unjustly, perhaps – as a perfect non-entity. A nine-to-five clerk in a municipal office, mired in stultifying routine, too stupefied even to resent it. Or maybe I see him that way because I want to, because it feeds my malice and my contempt, the only remaining components of my once complex emotional makeup.

"A wide subject," I grumble sourly.

"Listen. If you read the newspapers, and you look like someone who does, you probably know my name. Three years ago I – " A waiter abruptly materializes, and my guest breaks off to order a beer. The waiter looks at me, and I'm not quite sure what gesture I make, or whether I make any, but whatever it is it satisfies him, and with a slight bow he moves off.

"Three years ago I killed three people. Two small children and their mother."

He looks intently at me, as though to gauge how I'm taking this revelation, or confession, or whatever it is. He has counted on shocking me, of course, but I will not give him the satisfaction.

"It wasn't murder," he proceeds. "It was a car accident. I remember nothing about it. Nothing. I woke up one night – at least it seemed like night – in a place I didn't know, which turned out to be a hospital. How I got there, I had no idea until they told me, which wasn't until sometime later. I – "

"Excuse me."

"Yes?"

"Are you telling me this for a reason? And if so, does the reason have to do with me, or with you? Because if the latter – "

"You'd just as soon not know? Well, as to the reason, I confess that something in your face, I don't know what exactly, seemed to... well, I was struck by it. Here's a man, I thought, of sympathy and understanding."

"You're not skilled in the art of reading faces, that's obvious."

"No?"

"My sympathy, if I ever had any, dried up years ago. I'm sorry. Really, I can't help you."

"Forgive me for contradicting you. I think you can."

The waiter returns, setting a beer down before my guest, and a gin and tonic down before me.

"Try to imagine what it's like," he pursues, "to have done this awful, unspeakable thing, and yet... to remember nothing, nothing!"

"Waiter!"

The waiter pauses, turns to me with a quizzical look, and slowly, as though reluctantly, makes his way back to the table.

"I didn't order this."

"Beg pardon, sir, but – "

He's a man of about my own age who once told me, I think, that he was some sort of corporate big shot who took to waitering after retirement, not as a livelihood but as a hobby. Or maybe that was someone else.

"You certainly did order it," interposes my uninvited guest. "Come, don't give the man a hard time. It's all right," he says to the waiter. "You can go, I'll handle him."

Am I hearing this right? "You'll *handle* me? What exactly – "

"Please, sir, please. Calm down. All I ask is that you hear me out. The drink's on me. Please."

"But... who are you?" Too late I realize that my question has given him the opening he sought.

———

"Who am I? I'll tell you. I was nobody in particular, until my accident made me somebody. Nobody in particular... I had a job, a wife, children, a house, a mortgage... 'Nobody,' you see, means 'everybody.' I could have been anybody. I was good at my work, happy in my marriage, a loving father to my two kids, a dutiful son-in-law to my wife's mother... And then came... my accident. About that I can tell you very little. No more than what you must've read in the papers. I'd been working late, and was tired but not exhausted. I had *not* been drinking – that was established most definitely in court, to the satisfaction of all concerned. I had never had a car accident before. Never so much as a speeding ticket. And then... what happened that night? I know no more than what came out in the investigation: my car had somehow strayed into the lane of oncoming traffic. Had I momentarily fallen asleep at the wheel? I'll never know. And so... a young mother and two small children are dead because of me. Because of me, because of me! Well? Speak!"

"You are a madman!"

"A madman? Yes, in a sense. You can hardly have a thing like that happen to you and be entirely sane. And yet I carry on. After my acquittal – I was charged with negligence resulting in death – my company took me back, my wife remained the rock of support she has always been, my children, who were very small at the time, hardly seem to even know that anything is amiss – "

"Are you finished? May I – as we used to say in school – be excused?"

"I came to you because I thought you, as an older man, might have learned, and might teach me, that life is something other than a sick, perverse, cruel joke. It's a lesson I confess I am much in need of."

"Aren't we all!"

"You have read, of course, of the famous love-hotel murder."

"The famous love-hotel murder! No, I have not read of the famous love-hotel murder!"

"It's been in all the papers."

"I don't read the papers."

"I happen, you see to... well, to know the young woman."

"What young woman?"

"The woman who was killed. I know her, I... she worked in a supermarket; I used to... she worked at the cash. It's funny... I'd stop in on my way home from work, to pick up this and that... carton of milk, box of eggs... I always called home just before leaving the office, you see, and my wife would tell me what she was short of, and... there she'd be... I always lined up at her cash, even if another was less crowded, even if another cashier was entirely unoccupied. I guess... I don't know, it was kind of like a schoolboy crush I had on her, perfectly harmless, and yet, though we never exchanged so much as a word, those few minutes I spent in her vicinity... those few minutes were precious to me. Only once I did something... well, something a little mischievous. I don't know what possessed me. I handed her my business card and suggested she call me – oh! not for a minute thinking she would, just... as a kind of joke, you see. I never seriously thought she would call, never, and yet... it was possible! The possibility existed! And knowing it existed seemed to place my life on a whole new footing. I would lie awake at night, my wife sound asleep on the futon beside me, imagining the conversation we might have if she should happen, just for the hell of it, maybe in the same whimsical spirit in which I'd handed her the card, to call... And now... You are silent, you're not even looking at me, you haven't heard a word I've said... Well, it doesn't matter. You're right, I am a little mad..."

"You say she was murdered?"

"Murdered, yes, she and her boyfriend, in a love hotel room furnished, they say, like something out of the Arabian Nights, bludgeoned to death with an axe... an axe, can you imagine?"

"But... why?"

"No idea. A madman, I suppose. He's still at large, they haven't caught him. May I ask you a question?"

"What?"

"Do you believe in God?"

"Believe in God!"

"Yes, in an immaterial, inconceivable, ineffable spirit who created the universe and – "

"Are you – "

"Mad? We have already agreed that I probably am. Mad or not, I do believe in God. I'm not... I don't know whether the God I believe in is anything like the God of the Bible, Old Testament or New, but I believe in divine omnipotence, divine omniscience, divine justice."

"Divine justice! How can you... after the story you just told me..."

"Oh, of course, from our human, finite perspective – "

"All right, all right, enough of this! Enough! I didn't come here looking for company, and I've had more than enough of yours! Won't you... won't you please leave me alone at last?"

"Yes, it's high time I was off. My children will be waiting up for me, and I mustn't keep them up too late. Only... how is it, how is it, I wonder, that I was so drawn to you?"

"I can't imagine. Few people are, and though I don't come here often, when I do I generally have no trouble sitting undisturbed until I feel like going home."

"Isn't there something, something you can tell me? I'm sorry if I'm impertinent, but... a strange feeling I have that... you have something to tell me, something that could change my life, give it meaning."

"Meaning, eh? Meaning. All right, since meaning is what you're after, I will tell you something. Listen now. This very morning I woke up to find that I had left a burner on the stove burning all night. Just imagine. It's a gas stove. The building could have caught fire, and not only I but hundreds of others, men, women and children, nodding acquaintances and perfect strangers, could have been burned to death!"

"Terrible! May I ask you... has that ever happened before?"

"No, but it might again. What if I'm going senile? Eh?"

"Yes, it's a dreadful possibility, dreadful. My wife's mother, who lives with us, has Alzheimer's. She was such a lively, intelligent woman, and now she has to be prevented from eating her own toilet paper! But wait, let me ask you this: supposing.... supposing God appeared to you as He is said to have appeared to Abraham and Moses, and... this is blasphemy, perhaps... offers you a choice: to live on and on into advanced senility, or... or to be bludgeoned to death with an axe! Which would you choose?"

"The axe. Definitely I'd choose the axe. Definitely."

"Yes, I think I would too. So you see..."